SAMURAI KIDS

MONKEY FIST

SAMURAI KIDS

MONKEY FIST

SANDY FUSSELL

CANDLEWICK PRESS

Text copyright © 2009 by Sandy Fussell
Illustrations copyright © 2009 by Rhian Nest James

First U.S. edition 2012

Library of Congress Cataloging-in-Publication Data is available.

Library of Congress Catalog Card Number pending

ISBN 978-0-7636-5827-4

11 12 13 14 15 16 BVG 10 9 8 7 6 5 4 3 2 1

Printed in Berryville, VA, U.S.A.

This book was typeset in Garamond Three.

Candlewick Press
99 Dover Street
Somerville, Massachusetts 02144

visit us at www.candlewick.com

For Ben, Haydn, and Brittany
S. F.

For Tom and Sinead
R. N. J.

THE SAMURAI KIDS

KYOKO A girl with white hair, pink eyes, six fingers, and six toes. Her spirit is the Snow Monkey.

MIKKO A boy with one arm. His spirit is the Striped Gecko.

NIYA The boy with one leg who narrates the story. His spirit is the White Crane.

YOSHI A huge, strong boy who doesn't want to fight. His spirit is the Tiger.

TAJI A boy who is blind. His spirit is the Golden Bat.

NEZUME The last boy to join the Cockroach Ryu. His spirit is the Long-Tailed Rat.

THE TEACHER

SENSEI Also known as Ki-Yaga the wizard. He
was once a famous samurai warrior.

CONTENTS

CHAPTER ONE

真

KIDNAPPED

"Yoshi!" I call his name over and over, but the valley remains silent. Not even an echo. Yoshi is gone.

Three weeks ago, we were traveling back home from China. One morning we saw smoke rising from the White Tiger Temple, the place we'd just left. Yoshi turned back to help our friends Mei and Du Feng and the other Shaolin monks defend their home, and now I fear that he is fighting for his life as the temple burns.

I wanted to go with him, but Sensei shook his head. "Yoshi must go alone. He will attract less attention that way. Also, I know a man who can help him travel quickly, and this man owns only one horse."

So Yoshi left and I stayed behind.

Day after day, Mikko, Kyoko, Taji, and I trudged after Sensei, heading north toward the Great Wall. But I always look over my shoulder, searching the horizon for my friend. If only I knew where he was. Sometimes it aches to have one leg missing, but without my blood brother, I feel an even greater hurt.

"Come on, Niya." Kyoko pulls me away from the cliff side. "Yoshi will be back as soon as he can."

"But what if he needs me and I don't even know?"

She looks directly into my eyes and through to my heart. "You would know."

Deep within me, the White Crane nods in agreement.

"Time to eat," Sensei calls, and my stomach rumbles in answer.

Another long, tiring day has tucked itself under the mountain's edge. Kyoko hands out rice rolls and fruit picked from the temple orchards, while Taji distributes the blankets.

We huddle together. Not for warmth — the evening air is cool and comfortable after a day in the sun. Not for safety, either. Samurai kids are not afraid of the night, and the back road has been empty for days. We draw together because it feels good to laugh and talk. Then sleep tugs me close, and the moon dips its weary head in my direction.

Dark shapes cover my eyes. They stick their fingers in my ears and slap their ghostly gloves in my face. The White Crane screeches in fright.

I wake with a jolt from the nightmare, but I can tell

the danger isn't in my imagination anymore. It is real now. Somewhere close by.

"Taji," I whisper. It is the middle of the night, and it's pitch-black.

No answer. How can that be? Taji has ears like the Golden Bat, and my call should have woken him. Sensei should be stirring, too.

Fear takes hold of my stomach, twisting it tight.

"Master?" I say, a little louder.

Nothing.

"Mikko!" I'm yelling now.

Mikko's strong grip circles my arm. "What's wrong?"

"Something terrible has happened," I say. "I can feel it."

Sensei's words race through my head. *It's not what you can hear that matters, but what you cannot hear. It's not what you can see that is important, but what you cannot see.*

My eyes finally adjust to the darkness and I spy Taji and Sensei asleep. I can't see Kyoko anywhere.

I panic. "Where is Kyoko?"

"I can't wake Sensei!" Mikko presses his ear against our teacher's chest. "He's still breathing, though."

"I can't wake Sensei!"

I shake Taji, but he doesn't react, either. Bending toward his face, I smell familiar traces of valerian, hops, and poppy. It's an herbal combination Sensei sometimes has his patients inhale to make them sleep deeply.

"They've been drugged," I say. "It should wear off in a few hours."

"Are you sure?" Mikko asks.

I'm not sure when they will wake but I tell Mikko what I know. "Sensei often uses the same herbs. We'll just have to wait for them to wake up."

Although I recognize the herbs, I don't know how strong the mix was. It's hard to think when my brain is crammed with questions.

Who would do this to us? Bandits often lurk along the mountain paths, but why would they want to drug us? What wayside robber is clever enough to outwit Sensei? And most important of all, where is Kyoko?

A branch snaps and I hunch closer to Mikko. He feels the same fear. His breath is short and shallow, but it rasps as loud as my thumping heart.

The moon has painted the mountain with wolf hair brushstrokes of silver, gray, and black. Even the sharp eyes of the White Crane can't see far ahead through the gloom. Anyone could be hiding there. Maybe they are waiting for Mikko and me to go back to sleep so they can return to their unfinished business.

"We have to look for Kyoko," I say. "Maybe she woke up and confronted the bandits. She might be lying injured somewhere. You go that way and I'll head over there." I point to indicate directions. I don't really want to split up. But if Kyoko is hurt, we need to find her quickly.

"Be careful," Mikko says. "The bandits might still be here."

The night watches us search. Forest shadows taunt. Trees raise their arms to challenge us in ghostly sword-play. Bushes scratch my arms and knee. My crutch catches on tree roots. One branch swings to hit me in the face, and the salty taste of blood trickles into my mouth. I don't care. All I care about is finding Kyoko.

I listen hard but hear nothing. Not even an owl hoots. How far have I walked? Not far enough, since I haven't found Kyoko.

Then I hear soft footsteps moving toward me. I catch my breath, hoping it's her, but it's only Mikko.

"She's not here," he says. "No one is."

I don't want to admit it, but I know he's right. Kyoko is gone.

"I think someone has kidnapped her," I whisper, not wanting to say the words aloud. As if saying them makes them true.

"Why would anyone kidnap Kyoko?"

Miserably, I shake my head. "I don't know, but it's the only explanation that fits."

We make our way carefully back to the camp and huddle close.

"I don't understand why the kidnappers didn't drug *us*. Why only Taji and Sensei?" Mikko asks.

I think I know the answer to that one. "I was having a nightmare. I must have disturbed them when I woke and cried out."

"So we were the lucky ones," Mikko says.

But I don't feel lucky, and there's no way I can go back to sleep.

Mikko can't sleep, either. There are still more questions between us. "Who could possibly sneak up on Sensei?" he wonders.

I don't have an answer this time. Not even a ninja can slip by our master unnoticed. "Maybe Sensei will tell us in the morning," I suggest. If Sensei knows who stole Kyoko, he will know where to look for her.

"If he wakes up," says Mikko, looking away.

I'm glad he doesn't look me in the eye. I don't want him to see how worried I am. I think back through our master's teachings, looking for something that will help us now.

"Sensei always tells us that a cockroach is hard to kill. It will take more than a cowardly band of kidnappers to defeat him," I say.

"You're right," Mikko agrees. "Those bandits have made a big mistake. They have insulted Sensei's honor by abducting his student. A samurai will never rest until his honor is restored."

Mikko and I wait for the sun to crawl over the horizon and for Sensei and Taji to wake. It's hard to be patient when every minute means that Kyoko is farther away.

"Don't worry." Mikko wraps his one arm around me. "Sensei will know what to do, and Taji's nose can find a noodle in a haystack."

I hope Mikko is right. Together samurai kids can do anything, and surely that's enough to rescue Kyoko.

I just wish Yoshi were here to help.

CHAPTER TWO

仁

FOREST DEMONS

Sensei opens one eye to find me watching. He smiles and opens the other. "Good morning, Niya."

I'm relieved to see my teacher awake and well, but I am not interested in small talk. We have a big problem to solve. Urgently.

"There is nothing good about this morning," I say. "You and Taji were drugged last night, and Kyoko is missing. I think she has been kidnapped."

Sensei tips his head to one side, slapping his ear. Then he shakes his head back and forth. "First, I must clear the fog from my brain. I remember the smell of sleeping herbs and hearing Kyoko struggle. Then someone gave my skull a good clunk with a stout stick."

I begin my story with the nightmare and end with how it all came true. "And now Kyoko is gone."

"We looked everywhere for her," adds Mikko.

"Do not worry. All is not lost. Not even Kyoko." Sensei untucks his beard from his sash and stretches. "Now, where is my breakfast?"

Perhaps Sensei did not clear enough fog, after all. How can he think of food? My appetite is definitely lost, and Mikko feels the same.

"I'm not hungry," Mikko says. "Shouldn't we be packing so we're ready to go as soon as Taji wakes?"

"A samurai cannot travel far on an empty stomach." Sensei searches in his bag for last night's leftover rice rolls. "We must eat. We have many miles to cover in a short time."

"We could eat on the way. We could even carry Taji," I say, eager to set off. I trust Sensei's judgment, but I would feel a lot better if I was doing something to find Kyoko.

Sensei shakes his head, handing me a peach. "The foolish warrior rushes into battle, but he rarely rushes out. It is hard to run when you have left your head behind. I was caught unaware last night and will not repeat the mistake this morning."

I sigh. We're not going anywhere in a hurry.

Beside me Taji groans, struggling to sit up. "Where's Kyoko?"

Even without eyes, the Golden Bat is quick to see. Everyone smells different, he once told me, and I understand that. Kyoko smells like sweat and cherry blossoms.

"She's been kidnapped," says Mikko.

"What?" Taji yawns and rubs his eyes, forcing himself into wakefulness. "How did they sneak past us?"

And how did the bandits sneak past Sensei? Our master has eyes in the back of his head, and he doesn't even need to open them to see. He watches us practice at the *ryu* even when he is fast asleep, and he never misses a move. "More practice," he yells as soon as we think it is safe to stop and play.

"More eating," he commands this time, rolling a plum to each of us.

"Taji is awake now. Can we pack up and go? Please," I plead with Sensei.

"While you eat, I will tell you what I have concluded," our master says.

Reluctantly, I bite into the fruit. The flesh is sweet and the juice drips down my chin, tickling my neck. If only I could relax and enjoy it. But I don't want to waste any more time talking or eating.

Images of Kyoko, frightened and cowering, run through my imagination. My thoughts race after them. If anyone harms her, that person will answer to me. My hand moves to my sword for comfort, but it's not enough.

Sensei spits a plum pit into the grass. "I have lived a very long time, and it is much easier to make ten enemies than it is to make a friend. I have many enemies but only one lives here in northern China."

"Perhaps Qing-Shen followed us here," suggests Taji.

Qing-Shen was once Sensei's pupil, and now he is our master's sworn enemy. Yoshi beat him fair and square at the White Tiger Temple, but we don't trust him not to come hunting Sensei again.

"No." Sensei rubs the side of his head. "Qing-Shen would want everyone to see him triumph over me. He would not hide in the dark. I know who is behind this, and I have been expecting him to move against me. This man is a scholar and a player of games."

"What does he want then?" Mikko asks. "Why did he take Kyoko?"

"Lu Zeng wants to teach me a lesson, and he is using Kyoko to do it. Once we were friends, but he grew jealous of my success. He swore that one day I would regret ever knowing him."

"I knew lessons were nothing but trouble." Mikko rolls over in the grass.

It's true, learning is often boring and sometimes even a little dangerous, like when Taji breaks my nose during sword-fighting practice, but it's not life threatening. Now that Sensei's head is back to normal, we'll rescue Kyoko soon.

Still, the White Crane feels uneasy. What sort of man kidnaps a child to teach another man a lesson? Our Snow Monkey is just a playing piece in this scholar's twisted game.

Let's go now, I implore Sensei again. Deeper, inside where the White Crane worries.

Less haste, Little Cockroach. If we do not take the time we need, we will not have enough time to rescue Kyoko.

Kicking the pile of peach and plum pits out of the way, Sensei gestures to us to come closer. "When I was last in China, I studied for the Imperial Examinations. . . ."

We already know that. Sensei told us on the way to the temple.

"You came in first," Taji says proudly.

"Yes. I earned the title Jin Shi. It is a great honor."

"And it gives you the right to marry a princess." Mikko grins. Our lazy lizard likes to pretend he doesn't remember his lessons, but Mikko can remember things when he tries.

Sensei nods. "Lu Zeng studied for the tests, too. He felt that being outranked by a foreigner in the Imperial Examinations was an enormous disgrace. The years have increased his shame. It makes sense that he seeks to humiliate me by stealing one of my students and watching me fail to win her back."

"But where has he taken Kyoko?" I want to go there now, not sit listening to stories.

"She is on her way to the Forbidden City, the home of the Chinese Emperor and of Lu Zeng," Sensei says, shaking his finger at my impatience. "If we are lucky, we will catch the kidnappers before she is taken through the Outer City Gates."

"And if we don't?" asks Mikko.

"Then our task will be more difficult. Lu Zeng is a clever man, and in the palace, his words command."

"I am not afraid of a scholar who waves a brush and an ink pot," splutters Mikko, hand on his sword hilt.

But I am. Every time Sensei says Lu Zeng's name, the White Crane cringes.

"Is Kyoko safe?" I whisper the words, fearful of the answer.

"Lu Zeng will not raise a weapon against her. He needs Kyoko alive, at least until we meet face-to-face. But danger wears many disguises. The mind can be bound as easily as the body. If Kyoko's spirit holds strong, she will survive unharmed."

Sensei's words give me hope. Kyoko's spirit is as hard and sharp as the *shuriken* stars she throws, and her Snow Monkey fingers can undo any knots that try to hold her.

"Lu Zeng is a coward." Mikko clenches his one fist in anger.

"I agree. But he is also an esteemed Tao teacher and his students have very powerful ears. Even the Emperor holds him in great regard and sends his children to listen," Sensei says. "We will have to tread carefully."

"We will walk the way the Owl Ninja taught us," promises Taji.

You can't get any more careful than that. A ninja can creep across a bed of dry leaves, his footsteps blowing like the night wind. We'll sneak up and steal Kyoko back.

Taji cups his hand to his ear. "Yoshi is coming, and he's bringing horses."

Yoshi! That's good news. And horses will help us travel much faster. Hurrah! Finally we can go. Mikko and I hurriedly pack up the blankets as Taji grabs another piece of fruit.

Even I can hear the horses now.

I can't wait to see Yoshi. I want to hug my friend, dance around, and whoop with joy, but that would waste time we don't have.

When Yoshi clatters into our camp, we are ready, waiting to leave.

"What happened at the temple?" Taji asks. "Is Mei all right? And Du Feng?"

"Yes," Yoshi says. "The smoke we saw was a raid by army deserters. The monks had no trouble defending their temple." Dismounting, he notices everything stacked and ready to go. "These horses will need watering before we continue on."

"Where did the horses come from?" asks Sensei, his eyes narrowing with suspicion.

Perhaps he thinks Lu Zeng sent them. But I don't care as long as they can run fast.

"A strange thing happened when I was a day away from here. A man stepped out of the forest right in front me. As if he had materialized out of the mist," Yoshi says, waving his hands to demonstrate. "He gave me the reins and said that Elder Ki-Yaga needed horses in a hurry. Then he disappeared like that." Yoshi snaps his fingers. "I came as fast as I could. I'm starving. Is there anything to eat before we leave?"

Taji hands Yoshi a peach.

"The man only gave me five horses. I guess two of us will have to share." Yoshi looks around. "Wait. Where is Kyoko?"

"Sensei suspects that a scholar named Lu Zeng has kidnapped her," I say, hooking my pack onto the nearest horse. "He's trying to punish our teacher for beating him in the Imperial Examinations."

"Then what are we standing around for?" Yoshi asks.

I slap my friend on the back. "That's what I've been asking, too."

Yoshi and I always think alike.

But Sensei is still not ready to go.

"What did this man look like?" he asks.

Yoshi looks thoughtful. "I can't remember anything about his appearance, except that he was very ordinary. There was nothing to notice."

"To be no different from everyone else is a most effective disguise," Sensei says. "Are you sure he said *Elder* Ki-Yaga?"

"Yes. I thought it was because you are very old," Yoshi says, smiling. "And wise," he hastily adds. Sensei often teaches manners with a sharp clip around the ears from his *bo*.

But Sensei is not offended. He's grinning.

"I know who sent the horses," he says.

"Who?" we chorus. "Was it Lu Zeng?"

"Lu Zeng's men are common criminals. Those who stoop to steal children in the dark are not skilled enough to hide in light mist." Sensei snorts at the idea. "Who could be so cleverly disguised? Who could disappear like magic?"

Sensei is watching me, waiting for me to solve the puzzle. Suddenly the rice ball drops.

"Are there any Chinese ninja?" I ask.

"The ninja are everywhere in one shape or another." Sensei beams at me. "Here in the Land of the Dragon they are called forest demons, the Lin people. You will find them in the shadows at night. If you can find them at all."

I remember when Mikko and I were searching for Kyoko. It felt like the night had a hundred eyes. Maybe it really did.

"Are they on our side?" Yoshi asks hopefully.

Sensei shrugs. "I do not know. Their ways are difficult to understand. In the morning they might provide us with horses, and in the evening they might steal our food."

"Exchanging food for five horses would be a very good bargain. I would not begrudge them that," Taji says. "But if the Lin were watching us, why didn't they stop Lu Zeng's men from kidnapping Kyoko?"

"What if the Lin want to ensure we go to the Forbidden City?" I say. "They didn't rescue Kyoko so we would have to follow her there, and they sent us horses so we would arrive as quickly as possible."

Sometimes you surprise even me, Sensei whispers in my head. "The Lin are neither friend nor foe. It is true they have their reasons, and we will find out soon enough," he says.

"At least the temple is safe," says Mikko.

Yoshi shakes his head. "For now, but the abbot says it is the beginning of the end."

"Without imperial favor, the temple is an obvious target," Sensei says. "The army has long been nervous of the monks' fighting abilities. Soon the military commanders will turn their greedy eyes toward the temple and its treasures."

Now Yoshi is nodding. "The abbot has begun to send the monks away. Mei and Du Feng have already left."

"Where did they go?" I ask.

Yoshi hesitates, then looks at Sensei. "I don't know."

The White Crane stares at Yoshi. He is hiding something from me. And Sensei knows what it is.

What's wrong? I reach into Sensei's mind. *Tell me.*

There is nothing more to know, my master says. But inside his head is empty. As if he swept it clean before he let me in.

Don't be stupid, I tell myself. I must be imagining things because I am worried about Kyoko. Yoshi is more than my friend; he is my blood brother.

"No matter what happens, we carry the skills of Shaolin with us, and we will make sure they are never forgotten. There is nothing more we can do to help the monks," Sensei says. "We have our own mission to complete, and now we have horses to take us there."

Suddenly, the morning explodes into a thunderstorm of noise. Something falls from the sky and lands in front of us. Sticks jump and dance, spewing sparks. The valley echoes with huge whip cracks of sound, forcing us to cover our ears.

The horses spook and bolt into the forest.

Mikko hurries backward, dragging Taji with him. I follow. But Sensei stands firm beside Yoshi.

"Do not be afraid," our master says.

"They are firecrackers," explains Yoshi. "I saw them used at the temple. There they formed bright-colored patterns to entertain the audience."

"And here they risk setting fire to the forest just to attract our attention." Sensei uses his blanket to snuff the last of the sparks.

Stamping the smoldering grass, we make sure the flames don't flicker again. One of the cylinders has not burned. It is a metal container, the sort used to send important messages.

"Is it from the Lin?" I ask.

Suddenly, the morning explodes into a
thunderstorm of noise.

Sensei chuckles. "Most of the Lin people would consider learning to write a waste of time. Unlike the samurai, they do not write battle poems to celebrate their own deaths. They prefer not to die."

"I might join them," says Mikko. "That sounds very sensible to me."

Mikko hates calligraphy as much as I do. And no one wants to die. Not even a samurai kid. Many samurai warriors believe that to die with honor is the most important thing of all. Sensei teaches that it is much more important and much harder to live with honor.

Carefully, our master prods the container from the ashes with his traveling staff. "Bring some water, Mikko," he instructs him.

Hiss. Splt. The water sizzles against the hot metal until finally it is cool enough for Mikko to hand to Sensei.

Sensei undoes the cap and pulls a piece of silk from inside. It is shadowed with scorch marks now, but the dark, bold brushstrokes are still easily read. Even from here I can feel the tone. Loud. Insulting.

But our teacher is smiling.

"What does it say?" Taji asks.

"Lu Zeng has sent me a message. He has taken Kyoko

to the Forbidden City, as I expected, and he is challenging me to rescue her. It seems my esteemed opponent was worried I would not be able to work all this out for myself." Sensei returns the message to its container. "I have an advantage when he underestimates me."

We know what Sensei means. People underestimate us all the time. They think because we have an arm or leg missing or cannot see that we can't do things as well as everyone else. It's an enormous advantage.

Anyone who thinks Sensei's wits have dulled with age is in big trouble. Sensei's wisdom stretches farther than the North China Plain. His brain is sharper than the edge of his sword. And he has all of us to help him.

We want Kyoko back, and we won't allow anything or anyone to stand in our way.

But Lu Zeng's firecracker message has slowed us down. We can no longer leave right away.

We have to find our horses first.

CHAPTER THREE

名誉

FIRST GATE

"Found one," Yoshi calls.

"Me too," shouts Mikko.

Scrunch. Scrackle. Ahead of me I hear a sound in the undergrowth. I thought it would be hard to find five frightened horses in the forest. Here the trees grow thicker and the light dims with every step away from the path. But the sound leads me to a horse waiting impatiently for someone to untie the rope mysteriously tethering it to a tree.

No wonder the horses haven't strayed far. The forest demons wouldn't go to all that effort to give us horses and then let them run away. Approaching slowly, I hold out my hand.

"It's all right. I won't hurt you."

The horse looks at me with wary eyes. Sensei says animals can read voices the way we read characters from a parchment. They can tell a man's story from the roll of his words. This horse has decided he likes me. He nuzzles into my hand and sniffs at the dried peach and plum juice.

He is small and sturdy, with a coat that gleams dark brown with pale patches splattered here and there, as if someone dipped him in soy sauce but missed a few spots.

He seems to smile at me and flecks my shoulder with horse spit. I throw my arms around his neck and hold him close to breathe in the warm earth smell. We're part of the same story now. And as soon as we find Kyoko, it'll have a happy ending.

From the corner of my eye I see a small movement. "Who's there?" I call.

I hope it's a forest demon. Then I can say thank you and ask why they are helping us.

Nothing moves except for the horse, who is licking my hand clean.

But the White Crane sees like a ninja. It doesn't look for what is there; it looks for the shadows cast by what has just left to hide somewhere else.

"I'm a friend," I call. "Why are you hiding from me?"

The shadow crouches, smaller and smaller, lower and lower, until it melts into the forest floor.

"Thank you!" I yell as loudly as I can, sending my voice through the trees, just in case the demon can still hear me.

"What was all the shouting about?" Taji asks when I return with my horse.

Mikko rolls his eyes. "Niya just likes to yell."

"I think I saw someone. They must have tied my horse to a tree so I could find it easily."

"My horse was roped, too," says Yoshi.

"And mine," chorus Taji and Mikko.

Only Sensei didn't need any extra help. "Not my horse." He shrugs. "I whistled and she came."

Of course she would. Sensei is a legendary warrior of the days when samurai were men of the horse and bow. A good horse would sense that. And the forest demons would already know.

"Time to leave," Sensei says, climbing onto his horse. "The Lin and Lu Zeng are both waiting. Kyoko too."

He raises his traveling staff high, its crane and owl feathers flying in the breeze. *"Banzai!"*

Sensei's war cry fills the valley with the sound of his *ki.* It's more powerful than the noise of a thousand firecrackers. No one can keep Sensei from his student.

I raise my crutch and shout too.

"Aeeeyagh!" the White Crane screeches.

No one can keep Kyoko from me.

We chase hard and fast along the mountain path. Even Sensei is in a hurry now, and we don't stop for lunch or dinner. No one complains. Kyoko is far more important than an empty stomach.

The sun has burrowed deep into the ridge by the time Sensei gives the signal to halt. Early evening shadows drape across the peaks, their touch cool and refreshing after endless hours on horseback.

When I sit to rest beside Yoshi, I ask him about Mei and Du Feng again, just to see if I was only imagining things when I saw him hesitate earlier.

"I . . . um . . . I think I hear Sensei calling. I have to go," he mutters, avoiding the White Crane's gaze as he stands.

He *is* hiding something.

This is worse than just keeping a secret; my friend is lying to me.

"Yoshi!" Sensei calls. "I need help feeding the horses."

True friends trust each other. Do not be so quick to judge, Sensei whispers inside my head.

Sorry, Sensei. I hang my head. But deep down, I don't like the feeling of not being included.

Right now, though, I've got more important things to worry about. Where is Kyoko? Is she afraid? I wish I could wrap my arms around her and keep her safe. But I know that if I ever even suggested that, Kyoko would punch me in the arm.

Smiling, I close my eyes and send a message. *Be brave. We're coming as fast as we can.* I know she can't hear me the way Sensei does, but it makes me feel better.

The days blur into a routine of waking, eating, riding, and sleeping.

We keep our spirits bright by telling stories about old times. Monkeys call from the forest, and their chatter brings memories back to us. We use the memories to hide our worry from one another.

"Remember when Kyoko laced our bows to Sensei's cherry tree?" Taji reminisces.

Mikko groans. "It took all morning to untie them, and my hand ached for days."

Kyoko loves knots almost as much as playing tricks on us.

"Remember how on the boat to China, Captain Oong spent hours trying to teach us to tie the monkey-fist knot?" says Yoshi.

"He said, 'You boys have fingers like crab claws, but Kyoko's are light and gentle like a jellyfish trail,'" Sensei says, laughing.

The captain was right. More so than he realized. Jellyfish tentacles sting, and Kyoko's hands can be just as lethal. It's sad to think about the captain, and for a moment we fall silent. Three days from the coast of China, a great storm whipped the ocean. Captain Oong fell overboard and drowned. Even Yoshi was not strong enough to rescue him.

Yoshi blamed himself until the day he defended Sensei against Qing-Shen. A life lost. A life saved. That's how Yoshi's spirit found its balance again. But it took a long time, and it worries me when Yoshi looks sad.

I search his face now for reassurance that he's still okay. I'm relieved when he smiles at me, but I can't smile back. Not today.

"Hey, Niya, remember when Kyoko gave you two black eyes in a wrestling match?" Mikko pokes me in the side.

My friends guffaw at the memory, but there's no shame in losing to Kyoko. She's a champion wrestler and has beaten all of us many times.

Eventually, our laughter fades away, and in the silence, the nervousness in my stomach grows loud.

On the fourth morning, Sensei wakes us before the sun.

"What's wrong?" Mikko is instantly wide awake. If ever I go into battle, I hope Mikko is riding beside me. The Striped Gecko is always alert, ready for action.

"*Aaarh!*" Yoshi yawns, rolling onto his stomach. The battle would be over before Yoshi even got out of bed. But it probably wouldn't matter anyway. Yoshi doesn't like to fight, but he likes to plan. And he would have every step mapped out for us the night before.

I do trust Yoshi. And I trust Sensei, too. But I am starting to wonder if they trust me. Why won't they tell me about Mei and Du Feng? Why do they feel they need to hide things from me?

"It's still dark." Taji interrupts my thoughts. "Just after midnight, I would guess."

How does a kid who can't see know that? I have asked him before, and he said that telling the time is all about shadows. They are darker and harder to see at night. A shadow can betray many things.

Like when a forest demon is hiding from me.

Or when Yoshi turns his face away so he doesn't have to meet my eyes.

"We will be inside China's northern capital by sunrise," Sensei says. "Camped outside the walls are troops of soldiers, on guard to protect the palace from invasion and on call for war. A group of foreigners will arouse great suspicion, but if the soldiers are still asleep, we will not have to waste a day answering questions. We must sneak through to the main Outer City Gate."

"What are we waiting for then?" I demand.

Sensei tosses a piece of fruit in my direction. It's breakfast first.

"A traveling samurai must always eat. He never knows when he will find his next meal," he reminds me.

Mikko is eager to get going, too. Jumping around, he slashes with an imaginary sword, cutting a swathe into the city.

"Will we have any trouble passing through the gate?"

he asks. Eyes gleaming, Mikko would love a chance to demonstrate his swordsmanship.

"The jade seal I won in the Imperial Examinations is the key to many gates, including the one into Beijing. For once, we will be welcome."

Mikko sits with a disappointed thump. "Where is the fun in that?"

"We're not supposed to be having fun." I swing my crutch and he ducks. "We're supposed to be finding Kyoko."

"I have been here before and know where to begin looking," Sensei says. "Inside the northern capital is the Imperial City. At its center is the Forbidden City, a maze of *hutong* alleyways, barred buildings, and royal palaces. Kyoko will be in the middle, where everything important can be found. Do not worry."

But I am worried. The closer we get, the more I think about Kyoko being in danger. She could even be dead by now. Would Sensei know? I'm not brave enough to ask.

"What's wrong, Niya?" Mikko asks.

"Nothing really," I mumble. "Just a stomachache."

I feel as if my innards are made of bamboo and every

day, the grubs gnaw deeper. They'll feast and grow fat until I know Kyoko is safe.

"Chop, chop, Little Cockroaches." Sensei throws his pack onto his horse.

I hand him his traveling hat.

"Rar, rar," Yoshi roars and the horses charge forward.

Normally, I would ride with each of my friends in turn. And I still do, except I spend less time with Yoshi. I can't bring myself to ask again what I want to know and he won't tell me anyway. I don't feel like I can share my fear for Kyoko either. Instead, I talk about other things.

"Do you think Sensei has friends in the Forbidden City?" I ask.

Yoshi shrugs. "Maybe."

Our conversation drips then fades away. The silence cuts deep. Until it hurts. So I ride ahead to Mikko, to laugh and kick at his feet, pretending everything is all right.

When the trees grow less dense, Sensei slows his horse and dismounts.

"We cannot take animals into the city," he says. "In Beijing only the Emperor and his favorites may ride.

And even then it is not horses that carry them. It is other men." He loops a rope through the bridle and tethers it to a tree. "We will leave our horses here."

"Who will look after them?" asks Taji, stroking his horse's knotted mane.

Our master grins. "The same people who lent them to us. They were never ours to keep."

It's a welcome change to be walking again, although I will miss my horse's friendly whinny.

"We are not far from Kyoko now," Yoshi says, automatically reaching out to steady me when my crutch catches on a pebble.

The good memories we share flood back so fast that they would wash me away, except Yoshi is holding me in place.

"It's hard to be patient," I say.

And I'm trying to trust, I don't say. But Sensei hears it and nods approvingly in my direction.

In the distance we see the smudge of the soldier's encampment. As we draw closer, the camp sprawls like a tangle of kudzu vine between us and the Outer City Gate. Now I'm glad for all the times Sensei made us practice the thirty-three ways of walking. We'll need every trick we know to step quietly. Soldiers expecting an attack won't stop to ask questions of a group sneaking through their midst. This is much more dangerous than the Emperor's nightingale floor. One misplaced step and Kyoko will be left to wait forever.

Even asleep, the camp is alive with noise. Sighs. Coughs and wheezes. Snoring louder than a swarm of angry bees.

"Who does that sound remind you of?" Taji whispers.

"Niya," my friends answer.

"Sh!" Sensei cautions before I have a chance to protest.

Around the edges of the camp, early risers are awake, attending to the first duties of the day such as lighting the cooking fires, checking the perimeter, and watering the captain's horses. We sneak toward the middle of the hive, where no one is moving and the snoring is loudest.

We silently pick our way through the sleeping bodies. The air is warm and reeks of sweat, greasy plates, and urine. Soldiers lie with their arms splayed and their legs draped awkwardly across sleeping mats. Sometimes we have to jump over entangled limbs and equipment to find a space for our feet.

Ahead of me, Mikko stumbles and Yoshi catches his breath. But the Striped Gecko is more sure-footed than he looks, and he quickly recovers his balance. He turns to grin and wave at us. I bet he really wants to shout, "Ha! Scared you, didn't I?"

But then, as he takes his next step, Mikko crashes to the ground. I'm horrified to see a hand curled around his ankle. The soldier will raise the alarm and wake his comrades. Then we'll all be dead.

Sensei is so old, sometimes we hear his bones crack like thunder, but his reflexes are lightning quick. His sword is already suspended over the soldier's neck. Some threats are so loud, they don't require words.

I bite my lip. I don't want to see this man die. But if he doesn't, we will, and I want that even less.

Eyes wide with shock, the soldier freezes for a moment, unsure whether to scream or not. A moment is all Sensei needs. He drops to the man's side, thrusting his fingers hard against the soldier's neck. Wild eyes bulge and close. The man slumps, unconscious.

We've seen our master do this before. He'll wake up in a few hours, but by the time the soldier is repeating

Eyes wide with shock, the soldier freezes for a moment, unsure whether to scream or not.

and exaggerating this brush with death, we'll be inside the city.

The great lake of sleeping bodies tosses and turns. The ripple of movements runs like waves along China's coast. Small, careful steps take forever, but the hardest thing of all is keeping quiet.

As we reach the cleared area in front of the main Outer City Gate, the sun wakes slowly. It rubs its eyes and stretches rays across the sky. First pink, then red, and finally gold.

Above, the sneering walls of outer Beijing look down, daring us to enter.

The main gate is guarded by four soldiers in battle armor, lances in hand. Their dragon belts glitter in the early morning sun.

"It doesn't look like we'll be in and out in a hurry," Yoshi says, counting the watchtowers.

Sensei nods. "In the northern capital nothing happens quickly."

Even getting in with Sensei's seal is a complicated process.

"Name," demands the first guard.

"Ki-Yaga. Scholar of the First Class," Sensei announces.

"You don't look like a great scholar. Where is your Wu Sha hat?" the guard challenges. "I thought first-class scholars lived in palaces in the Forbidden City, wearing brocaded robes and drinking tea from a silver tray." He stabs his finger at Sensei's chest. "You, old man, look more like a traveling peddler. Someone who might try to sell me a cracked rice bowl."

We stand with our hands on the hilts of our swords, ready to defend our master's honor. But Sensei's glance tells us to wait.

"Nothing is ever quite what it seems, and many a cracked rice bowl is mended with gold lacquer. You would not be able to afford such a dish, but I will give you this advice for free." Our teacher swings his staff like a sword, and all four guards take a step back. "A man can learn more from a day sitting in the marketplace than he can from a year studying books."

Sensei moves closer to rap the first guard's helmet with his staff. "I bet my cracked bowl that this humble peddler is worth more than three palace scholars."

"You talk and act like a scholar." The guard glares.

"How do I know you are not just a good performer?"

Sensei passes his imperial jade seal over for authentication. "Perhaps this will speak for me."

"State your business, then," grunts the guard, handing back the seal. "It will need to be important. The walls of Beijing were closed to foreigners last month. Even educated ones."

"I am here to seek an audience with Lu Zeng."

"Then I will give *you* some free advice. When one speaks the name of Lord Lu Zeng, Esteemed Secretary of the Board of Rites, he must do so with proper respect. Otherwise he will find himself in the Emperor's prison, learning better manners."

"My humble apologies. I did not realize how far my old friend had ascended," says Sensei, bowing ever so slightly. "Maybe he will not remember this worthless one, after all."

Nodding, the guard approves our master's show of respect. But we know better. It was barely a bow at all and, in Japan, that's an insult.

"Friends of the Esteemed Secretary are always welcome. As long as they are on the list." The guard holds up a long scroll. "What did you say your name was?"

"I am Ki-Yaga, a teacher from across the sea. These are my students."

Rummaging in the locker behind him, the second guard produces a container like the one Sensei has in his pocket, except this one isn't charred and sooty. It is covered with purple brocade and embroidered with orange silk. It must be worth a small fortune.

"I apologize for my earlier questioning, Jin Shi Ki-Yaga. In these times of unrest, a sentry must be very careful." With an exaggerated flourish, he hands the container to Sensei. "You are indeed expected. Secretary Lu Zeng has left a personal message for you."

"I understand," Sensei says. "I will commend you to the Esteemed Secretary."

All four guards salute. The Outer City Gate opens, and Sensei, now a person of importance, strides through. Mikko, Taji, Yoshi, and I scurry after him.

"Welcome to Beijing, the greatest city in the world," one of the guards calls after us.

There's nothing great about it so far. Except that we are

closer to Kyoko. We hasten along the tunnel, wondering how many spying eyes peer from side alcoves. It's not safe to talk freely yet.

Out in the sunshine, we crowd around as Sensei takes a scroll from the container.

"What does it say?" I ask.

"It is a list of the Twelve Symbols of Sovereignty. Lu Zeng has given us a puzzle to solve. Once we reach the Forbidden City, these clues will lead us to Kyoko."

I follow our master's pointed finger. My hearts sink. The Forbidden City means more gates, walls, watchtowers, and guardhouses. We're barely inside the capital. All we've done is peel away one thin layer of rice paper.

"What's the first clue on the list?" asks Taji.

"It's sun," Yoshi reads aloud over Sensei's shoulder.

I look up. My eyes are blinded by the sun's return gaze.

That's no help at all.

CHAPTER FOUR

忠誠

UNDERGROUND

"Ripe plums!"

"White rice unloaded only yesterday! Guaranteed no weevils!"

"Slippers fit for an emperor!"

Around us the street vendors wave their arms, pointing theatrically to their wares.

But the show is wasted on us. We have no money to buy anything, not even half a pair of slippers for me.

A grubby man in tattered sackcloth sidles up to our master. "Can I interest you in something, elder one? Perhaps a new robe. The one you wear is old and dirty."

As if he should talk.

But Sensei smiles, encouraging. "Maybe you can help me. I am looking for the Twelve Symbols of Sovereignty. I have heard they can be found inside the Forbidden City."

The peddler laughs.

"What's so funny?" I ask.

"The idea that anything valuable would be found in the vicinity of a palace."

"But the palaces are full of riches. I have heard of pearl mirrors and roofs paved with gold," Mikko insists.

Even Taji can imagine the treasure. "Silver dinner sets and jade placemats."

"And huge statues set with ruby eyes," adds Yoshi.

The man laughs even louder.

"Perhaps something of great value can be found here in the marketplace," Sensei suggests, moving closer to stare deep into the peddler's eyes.

I know that feeling. Sensei's gaze can drill all the way through to a man's heart. But this man is not worried. He stares back. He has nothing to hide.

The peddler laughs again, gesturing Sensei even closer. He whispers into our master's ear.

Sensei nods.

"What's he saying?" Mikko asks Taji.

"If we meet him in the shadow of the Temple of Agriculture at first darkness, he will show us where to find what is truly valuable," repeats Taji.

My heart does a somersault, waking the White Crane. The peddler must be talking about Kyoko. Sensei would not be interested in anything else.

Edging away, the man fades into the fringe of the crowd. It folds around and over him. One moment he is there, and now he is not.

"Are we going to meet with him tonight?" Yoshi asks Sensei.

Sensei smiles and looks at Taji. Our teacher approves of listening in. A samurai needs to be prepared. It is the best way to ensure that your head stays where it belongs.

"I believe that man may be able to help us," says Sensei, tucking his beard into his sash.

"Why?" Mikko is suspicious.

And I am too. But I'm desperate to free Kyoko, even if it means trusting a stranger.

"There is always a bargain to be struck. Perhaps he thinks we can assist him," Sensei says. "We will soon find out."

I don't think there's much we can do to help a street vendor, unless it involves frightening someone who owes him money. I grin. That would be fun. I haven't drawn my sword for many days, not even in practice.

The street is filling with people. Buyers and sellers and others like us, just looking. Sensei threads his way through the crowd and we hurry to follow in his footsteps.

"I can give you the Twelve Symbols of Sovereignty." A voice crackles at my side.

Surprised, I stop suddenly, and Mikko walks straight into me. Yoshi and Taji halt just in time.

"What are we stopping for?" complains Mikko.

I gesture to the old man, his mouth gaping in a toothless grin. How did he know what we were looking for? He couldn't possibly have overheard our conversation with the peddler. Not even Taji could hear from that far away.

This stick-figure man, stooped almost double, is even thinner than Sensei. If he tried to straighten up, he would probably snap in two. His skin is ridged like cherry-tree bark, and his words rustle like dry leaves. "Would you like to see the twelve symbols?"

I nod.

From under his cloak he produces a robe. With a shake, it unfolds to display pictographs stretching from shoulder to ankle, richly embroidered in burnished thread. The sun, the moon, and three stars shine on night-blue silk. A dragon and phoenix soar over the mountain. Goblets glitter. Red-gold fire blazes above a bed of green seaweed and scattered grain. A bronze ax head gleams.

Beside me Yoshi gasps. Mikko whistles and Taji

reaches out to touch the fabric. His fingers slide along the silk, stopping at a strange Chinese symbol.

"That's *fu*," the man says. "The power to distinguish between right and wrong. Only a great man can do that. Like our Emperor."

Or Sensei.

Our master needs a new cloak, and this is the one he deserves to wear. I imagine how commanding he would look, standing before Secretary Lu Zeng, the Twelve Symbols of Sovereignty flowing from his outstretched arms.

"It's beautiful," I sigh. "I wish I could buy it for my teacher, but I have no money."

"This robe is not for sale." It vanishes back into the folds of the man's cloak. "Return here after you have rescued the boy, and I will give it to you as a reward."

And then, like the robe, the man disappears. I peer into the crowd, but even the White Crane cannot see through layers of flesh and bone. He is gone.

"That was strange," says Taji.

Mikko rolls his eyes. "And even stranger, he knew why we were here, but he got one thing wrong. We're rescuing a girl, not a boy."

"Kyoko could easily be mistaken for a boy," Yoshi says. "Especially if her face was hidden."

It makes me angry to think of Kyoko bound and bundled, although I smile to think they'd have to gag her, too. Kyoko is expert at throwing *shuriken* stars but she's just as good at hurling insults. We've all been on the receiving end of those sharp points.

"Come along," Sensei calls from up ahead. "No man ever traveled far by standing still."

"After we rescue Kyoko, we'll find our way back here," I say to the others.

Mikko points to a great stone fish arching skyward, water spurting from its mouth. "We just need to look for the fountain nearby."

It's a good sign. A leaping carp means good fortune will follow. Hopefully, it follows us all the way to Lu Zeng and Kyoko.

"Chop, chop!" Sensei calls again.

Our master doesn't like to be kept waiting. We hasten in the direction of his fading voice.

"These streets are the home of clever pickpockets," says Sensei when we catch up to him. "We must be careful."

"I'm safe from thieving fingers." Taji grins, turning out his empty pockets.

We all are. Only Sensei has anything of value, but the jade seal is hidden safely in the end of his traveling staff.

Still, trouble always finds its own way. A small hand snakes toward the hilt of Mikko's sword. Fortunately, Sensei strikes faster.

He grabs the thin wrist and pulls the boy toward him. "You are very lucky," he says.

"How can I be lucky?" The street urchin spits at our teacher's feet. "I got caught, didn't I?"

"Do you know what the penalty is for touching a samurai sword?" I ask.

The boy shakes his head, defiant.

"It is death," I say.

Sensei nods. "Even I could not save you from that. It is our law."

Surrounded by our solemn faces, the boy realizes the danger. He looks down, shuffling his feet against the cobblestones. "Sorry," he mutters.

"Is there a problem here?" The soldier's voice booms loud enough to part the crowd, and he strides through the gap. He's a big man with a great broadsword hanging from his waist. No one wants to argue with that.

All eyes turn toward us as the soldier assesses the situation. "We don't tolerate petty criminals on the streets of Beijing." He glares at the boy. "And we treat the Esteemed Secretary's guests with special respect."

Word travels through the city much faster than we do.

The soldier turns to Sensei. "This one's face is very familiar. It might do him good to spend a night in the Emperor's prison. Perhaps Secretary Lu Zeng will visit him there and teach him some respect."

At the mention of Lu Zeng's name, the boy turns pale. The White Crane is not the only one who fears Lu Zeng.

"No harm has been done, so no action is necessary," says Sensei firmly. "We were just describing our home in Japan. The boy would like to travel there someday."

"Not likely." The soldier guffaws. "An urchin like him couldn't afford the shoes to walk there." He moves off, still laughing at his joke.

"You should feel lucky now," Yoshi says to the boy. "You have been saved twice."

The boy nods. "And I *will* go to Japan. I'll show him. Stupid soldier. You can't even walk there, anyway."

"Perhaps you will travel on a boat." Sensei smiles. "No man can tell another where life's path will take him. If you do cross the sea, ask for directions to the Cockroach Ryu. You will be most welcome."

"Thank you," the boy murmurs before running off. He looks back and waves.

"Are you collecting new students?" asks Taji with a smile.

"I never know where a student will be found. Usually *they* find me." Sensei looks thoughtful, as if he is already miles away in our classroom in the Tateyama Mountains.

I wish I was there, too. Home safe with Kyoko. And Taji and Mikko. And the old Yoshi.

Moonlight bathes the city in pale silver. Every evening the day's grime is painted over, hidden until the morning sun peels it off again.

Like a row of ducks, we straggle behind our teacher. Yoshi and I are at the end of the line. Finally, it's the perfect time to ask again. He can't get away from me now.

"You know where Mei and Du Feng went to, don't you?" I ask as casually as I can, as if I only just thought of the question and haven't been thinking about it for days.

Sensei is clever with words and can build barriers quickly. Not Yoshi. Yoshi's strength is in his arms and his strategies, but I'm not giving him any room to maneuver this time.

"Sometimes it is better not to know something," he mumbles. "You should mind your own business, Niya."

"Why can't I know?" I persist. "What makes you so special?"

Yoshi's mouth is clamped shut, and he refuses to answer. Angry, I drop behind him. I may as well be alone.

The far corner of the Temple of Agriculture is draped in shadow. I can't see anyone waiting for us. But the Golden Bat can.

"They are already here," Taji whispers.

"Where?" Mikko asks, looking around.

Sensei points to a group of tallow trees. The wind rearranges the leaves, and the shadows shift with them. It's an excellent place to hide.

"We should announce our arrival," Yoshi suggests, gathering up pebbles and passing them around.

I'm too angry to talk to him and much too angry to admit that it's a good idea.

Taji does it instead. "Confucius said, 'Aim for the stars and you might hit the moon.' I think he would agree that anyone lurking in the dark is just as good a target."

Sensei raises his arm and drops it with a sharp stroke. His permission given, a volley of stones falls like a shower of rain into the cluster of shadows. Almost immediately, the others slink away and the first peddler we encountered emerges alone, walking toward us. Tonight he looks more like a ninja than a street vendor. He is wearing a dark bodysuit, and only his eyes are visible.

But that's enough. They are the eyes that convinced Sensei to trust him in the first place.

"Follow me," instructs the peddler.

"Do you have a name?" Sensei inquires.

"Not one that you have yet earned the right to use."

Sensei shakes his head when Mikko's hand moves to his blade. Our teacher is not insulted. He understands. A samurai values his name almost as much as his sword.

Our guide leads us down a narrow, high-walled *hutong* alley. It smells of people, dogs, and cooked cabbage. One street merges into another until I have no idea where I am. Sensei said the Forbidden City is like a great maze. We haven't reached it yet, and I am already lost.

Finally, our guide stops in front of a small house with a paved courtyard. Opening the gate, he climbs the stairs to rap twice on the door. It creaks slowly ajar. The hallway is empty.

"Hurry," calls our guide, already halfway along the narrow, gloomy corridor. "Help me with this mat," he says to Yoshi.

The rolled-up mat is old and worn but still heavy. When Mikko adds his strength, they manage to move it enough to reveal a wooden hatch. Beneath the raised hatch, a long line of metal rungs disappears into the darkness.

Mikko leans over to look. "I'm not going down there."

He doesn't like heights, in any direction—up or down.

"Everyone must enter," our guide insists.

Mikko shakes his head.

"I will keep you safe," Sensei promises him. "Our *obi* sashes will make a harness to tie us together."

Normally, that would be Kyoko's job. When Kyoko braids two strands together, they never come undone. I hope Sensei's knots are just as tight.

"We must hurry." Our guide gestures impatiently at the opening.

Yoshi goes first, climbing bravely down into the void. Taji next, then me, with my crutch strapped to my chest. Mikko and Sensei are farther behind.

Thunk! Above us, the hatch slams shut.

It's dark. Close and suffocating.

Samurai kids are not afraid of the darkness, but the idea of falling into a bottomless pit scares me stiff as a bamboo board.

"Do not fear." Sensei's voice cuts through the dark, every word a bead of light. "Think of Kyoko waiting for us."

I'd do anything for her, but it's not easy to stay calm. Our guide has just sealed us underground. We might even die entombed here. I bet others already have.

In my mind the walls move closer, pressing against me. Skeleton fingers reach out to poke my stomach. Below me Taji gasps. Even without sight, he feels the blackness as much as I do.

"Breathe deeply," our master intones.

Om-om, we chant until the tunnel is filled with the sound of our *ki.* The White Crane screeches, and the Tiger roars. The rattle of bones fades from my mind.

"We are in no danger. This is just a test," Sensei reassures us. "Our new ally needs our help and in return he will aid us. First, we must prove we are worthy. We must prove we are not fearful."

"But I prefer to see when I take a test," I complain.

"Why should you have an unfair advantage? I never get to see what's going on." Taji makes us snicker.

"I would prefer not to take a test at all," says Mikko with a groan.

Everyone laughs then.

Laughter has a way of changing things. It takes what

is fearsome and unknown and molds it until it is tame and familiar.

Slowly placing each hand and foot, we continue down.

"The rungs are damp here," Yoshi calls upward. "Careful, it's slippery."

We go even slower. Below me I hear Taji scramble as he loses his footing.

"Take my hand and jump," Yoshi says. "It's just soft earth below."

Thump. Taji lands safely.

I'm next, but when Yoshi holds his hand out to me, I brush it away. I don't need help. Especially not from Yoshi. Not today.

I stretch my crutch forward, placing it in a safe spot. With a great heave, I swing myself off the ladder. My crutch slips out of my hand.

Ayeeeagh! the White Crane screeches in panic.

I land in a crumpled heap at Yoshi's feet. As I rise, pain shoots through the ankle I injured on my way to the White Tiger Temple. I've hurt it again. All because I was too proud and too foolish to accept Yoshi's help.

"It's all right, Niya," Yoshi says. "I'll carry you."

With a great heave, I swing myself off the
ladder. My crutch slips out of my hand.

"I'd rather crawl," I whisper, my voice gritty and gruff.

Yoshi knows why. He can feel the edges in my voice, rough with the tears I'm holding back.

"What happened?" Mikko calls from above.

"Niya fell," answers Yoshi. "He's hurt his ankle again."

"I thought I could climb down myself," I interrupt before Yoshi says anything else. I don't want my friends to know that I put my pride first.

But Sensei will know. Nervously, I wait for him to lecture me. His tongue can be sharper than his sword, and it cuts even deeper. I'm lucky this time.

"Have you learned your lesson?" is all he asks.

"Yes." I hang my head miserably.

It's not quite true. I'm still unhappy with Yoshi.

"Yoshi will carry Niya," Sensei decides. "We will see what damage has been done to his ankle when we reach the end of the tunnel."

"I'm all right. I don't need help," I protest.

Sensei's glare silences my argument as Mikko and Taji help me climb onto Yoshi's back.

"The end of the tunnel will not be far away," says

Sensei. "This is an underground connection used to travel between safe houses."

The air is bitter with the faint smell of dead animals. It seems the tunnel stretches before us, dark and dank, forever.

The White Crane is a creature of light, of wide-open blue skies. The people in the village below our *ryu* gossip that Sensei is really a creature of darkness, a *tengu* demon that can change into a great black bird. Sometimes I wonder if there is any truth to these tales. Sensei can do amazing things. He knows about things before they happen. So maybe he does know where the tunnel ends.

But if Sensei is a *tengu*, it means he once did something truly awful. And that can't possibly be right.

"Uh-oh." Yoshi stops.

The tunnel, like a giant snake, has tapered into a forked tongue.

"Which way should we go?" Mikko asks.

"Hmmm." Sensei kneads his beard with both hands. He likes a puzzle, and normally I do, too. But I just want to get out of this tunnel and find Kyoko.

"We must be very careful. This is the place where

we pass or fail our test. And if we fail, we will not be allowed to leave here," Sensei says. "We already know too much."

That might be true, but we don't know enough.

We don't know which tunnel to choose.

CHAPTER FIVE

義

THE LIN PEOPLE

"I wish Nezume were here," I say.

Rat Boy wouldn't hesitate. He reads mazes as easily as any ordinary map, but he is back in Japan, serving as the personal swordship tutor to the Emperor's son.

"Yes, Nezume would know which way to go." Sensei scratches his ear.

Can you ask him? I speak into the wizard's head. *Can you call to him like this?*

No, Sensei says. *Can you?*

I've never tried, I answer, surprised. If Sensei can't do it, what chance do I have?

Try now, he suggests.

I close my eyes and concentrate hard. *Nezume.* I call down the Dragon's back and across the ocean.

No answer. Of course not. Japan is much too far away.

One day, Sensei whispers. *One day you will reach even farther than that.*

"We will go right," Sensei decides. "When in doubt, the right path is always the right way."

We all hope he's right about that.

"I can hear something," Taji says.

Sensei peers into the gloom. "I can see light glimmering ahead."

The White Crane has excellent eyes, too. But no matter how hard I try, the shadows all look the same to me.

I try to focus again. The shadows flicker. Along the wall, a shape creeps and dissolves.

"I saw someone," I exclaim in triumph.

If I could run, or even hop, I'd chase after them.

"We are being tested. How will anyone know we passed if there are no examiners watching our progress?" Sensei smiles. "Like the forest, this tunnel has many eyes."

And they're all spying on us. My friends don't like that any more than I do.

"Come out and show yourself!" roars Yoshi, swinging around and almost knocking my head against the tunnel wall.

"You can't hide from us. Even I know you are here," Taji calls.

"We can all see you," yells Mikko.

The noise echoes down the passageway, a shout of defiance. "We are not afraid," I yell.

"Come out and show yourself!" roars Yoshi.

Silence swallows our challenge, but our shadows grow large as the darkness dims. We walk twice as tall as before.

Have courage, Kyoko. We're coming to save you.

At the end of the tunnel is a door, but there's no bolt, no lock to open, not even a knob to turn.

"It's jammed shut," says Mikko, running his fingers around the edge, searching for a handhold in the gap between the door and wall. "We're trapped."

Maybe this wasn't the right fork in the tunnel, after all.

"*Hmph.* Doors exist only to be opened. You just need to know how." Sensei raps against the wood with his staff.

The door opens to reveal the peddler's smiling face. "Come in, come in." He waves us through.

I poke Mikko in the side. "How come you didn't think of knocking?"

"I didn't need to. I'm an expert swordsman," he boasts. "I could have chopped the door down."

"We probably wouldn't be very welcome then,"

mutters Taji. "People don't like it when you break down their secret entrances."

A large lantern swings from a hook in the middle of the roof. In the wavering light I count ten men. Their faces are sun browned, but their night-black eyes pick us apart with short, sharp stabs, the way a raven pulls the flesh from the bones of a dead mouse.

Half hidden by the corner shadows, an old man rises from a low bamboo chair. He has the darkest, beadiest eyes of all, and they are staring straight into our master.

"Perhaps your young students would like to wait in the next room while we talk."

Sensei shakes his head. "I am sure that whatever you have to ask involves them as much as me."

"How do you know we have something to ask?" The raven man moves slowly, dragging his leg like a broken wing. His body is frail, but his voice is strong and commanding.

"This morning I was offered information. I am sure you are aware I have no gold to pay," says Sensei. "I expect you have already determined another price."

The man laughs. Two chairs are placed beside him and he gestures for Sensei to sit. Yoshi lowers me to the ground and we all sit cross-legged in front of the two old men.

"Your master is very clever," he says to us. "Perhaps everything they say about him is true."

"What do they say?" I ask, intrigued.

"They say Ki-Yaga wields his sword like a lightning bolt," answers the man who opened the door for us.

"They say his war cry rolls louder than thunder, and, as with the summer monsoon, nothing is left standing after he passes through," says another.

Sensei shrugs. "That was a long time ago. I am a teacher now, training my students to fight in the hope they will never need to."

The old raven man leans closer. "Yet still you have never lost a battle. You have found other ways to triumph over your opponents." His voice drops to a whisper. "I have heard that you fly though the night like a great batlike bird with a long tail. And that no man can hide anything from you."

Raising my eyebrows at Mikko, I nudge Taji with my crutch. Even in China they have heard the stories about our teacher. I try to catch Yoshi's eye, but he's too busy studying the peddler.

Sensei scratches his chin. "Do you believe everything you hear?"

The old man's eyes are too dark for me to read. "I believe many things," he says. "I believe you can help me and I can help you."

"You already have." Yoshi points across the room. "This man is the one who gave me the horses. I didn't recognize him in the street today, but his gestures are familiar tonight."

"So you know who we are?" the old man asks.

"No," Yoshi says.

But I do.

"You're the forest demon I saw in the woods," I blurt out.

The man nods. "We prefer to be known by our own name. We are the Lin, an ancient race of the Chinese forest. There are no demons among us. Our skills are not supernatural but well practiced. I am Wan Dei, or Elder Lin, the eldest voice of our people. When I speak, we all speak."

"Thank you, Elder Lin," Sensei says, bowing deep. The formal gesture is heavy with respect. "I am grateful for your assistance, but you have not told me what you require of us. I assume you did not prevent my student's kidnapping because you desired us here for some other task of your own."

"You are right. When we heard what Secretary Lu Zeng was planning, we knew it would ensure that you came here. We provided horses to hasten your journey and have located the girl you seek. In return, we ask you to also rescue the boy the Secretary has imprisoned with her. His name is Enlai, and he is my grandson."

The old man in the street with the beautiful robe was right. There is a boy to be rescued.

Sensei tugs at his beard, curling it around his fingers. "Why haven't your people rescued him already?"

"We have tried," Elder Lin admits. "We can sneak into Secretary Lu Zeng's palace, but we cannot find where Enlai is hidden. We need your help to do that."

"Why does Lu Zeng want your grandson?" asks Mikko.

"The Lin live much longer than other Chinese people, and Secretary Lu Zeng intends to use Enlai to discover why."

"What can a boy tell an old man about such things?" Sensei snorts. "Lu Zeng would find more answers in his books and experiments."

A voice booms from the shadows at the back of the room. "Secretary Lu Zeng is not going to ask, and Enlai cannot speak anyway. He has been mute since birth. The Secretary is going to cut Enlai open and search his entrails for answers," the big man continues. "Enlai is the Secretary's next experiment."

Taji gasps. He might be blind, but that doesn't mean he can't see the grisly picture inside his head. My stomach churns. Just because Lu Zeng isn't a swordsman, that doesn't mean he's not dangerous.

"I thought human dissection was forbidden in China." Sensei's eyes flash with anger and something else—the realization that losing this new game might cost Kyoko her life. "The man I remember at least obeyed the rules of learning. It seems that has changed."

"Secretary Lu Zeng is old and desperate. He respects nothing," says the peddler. "Some say an illness eats away at his flesh. I say it feasts on his soul."

"Or his poisonous heart." A new voice spits words onto the floor with a snake's venom. The man who moves into the center of the room is large enough to dim the lantern light, casting us all into shadows. "Secretary Lu Zeng is a monster. Barely human."

"But surely he is not above the law." Yoshi clenches his fists.

Elder Lin sighs. "Who will miss one less boy running in the streets?"

Or a samurai girl no one even knows exists. Kyoko might be in great danger. Every second counts. I tug at Sensei's sleeve. "We've got to find them now."

"We will rescue them both as quickly as possible." Sensei bows again to Elder Lin. "I give you my word."

It's a valuable gift, and the old man recognizes its worth. He presses his hands together, dipping his head in thanks.

"The Emperor has declared three days of cleansing. During this time, no meat may be eaten and no blood of any kind spilled. Even Secretary Lu Zeng would not dare disobey the Emperor. For the moment, our children are safe from his knife," advises the old man.

"Lu Zeng has given me a list of clues to follow. But I will not play games with the lives of children. I will make my own rules."

Sensei's hand is on his sword, and his eyes are full of fire.

Lu Zeng is in big trouble now. Sensei is not preparing to teach a lesson. The warrior Ki-Yaga is readying himself for battle.

"First, you must know that the Secretary has hired an assassin to kill you," Elder Lin says. "Just in case you win. If you triumph, he will strike you down."

Sensei doesn't seem surprised to hear that. "Lu Zeng always was a sore loser."

"How do you know about the assassin?" Yoshi asks, his eyes glaring with suspicion. He doesn't trust the Lin yet.

"Secretary Lu Zeng asked me to arrange your master's death. Even in the palaces of the Forbidden City, our skill with potions and poisons is feared."

"I'm glad you said no," says Mikko.

"But I didn't." The old man smiles. "I said yes, that the axman, Big Wu, would do it."

The huge man still standing in the middle of the room nods. He wouldn't need poison. Or an ax. His great hands could break Sensei in two like a dead branch.

The old man continues. "I told the Secretary that if

he released our boy, then I would assassinate Jin Shi Ki-Yaga. But when he would not return Enlai, I refused. I will help you instead."

I wonder if the Lin gave Lu Zeng the sleeping potion his men used on us. They were playing on both sides then.

How can we trust someone who was willing to kill you? I ask Sensei.

I trust someone who is willing to tell me such a thing. The Lin think differently, Sensei reminds me. *More than anything else now, Elder Lin needs us to stay alive and rescue his grandson. We must work together and not be distracted by their secrets. After all, everyone has secrets. I have many of my own.*

The word *secrets* drops heavily into my heart. Across the room, Yoshi smiles at me. I know my friend well enough to read the lines of hope in his face. He desperately wants me to smile back.

Despite his secret, we must work together, too. For Kyoko's sake. When I force myself to grin and wink, a look of relief washes over Yoshi's face.

"We have sent our women and children into the forest," says Elder Lin. "When Enlai is returned to us, the last of the Lin will leave this city forever. We will not be here when it falls." The man's face melts into wistfulness and his gaze sweeps us all together. "Enlai is a special child. People assume that because he has nothing to say, he has nothing to think. They are mistaken. I know you understand."

We do. People always judge us by what they think we can't do, and they get it wrong all the time.

"We appreciate your help and advice," our master says. "But I already know where to find Kyoko. If you want me to rescue your boy, you must offer something more."

What? We would rescue a boy without payment. A samurai does not wield his sword for gold; he wields it for honor. And there is much honor to be gained here.

"What do you want?" The old man's black eyes are harder now. The raven has returned.

"Teach my students the ways of the forest. The techniques of camouflage and tracking and your skill with poisons. I also require a salve for Niya's twisted ankle. Without his help, I cannot rescue Enlai."

The tone in the room changes. I can feel it like an icy swell moving through the ocean. I shiver, taking a deep, cold breath.

"The salve will be provided, but I will have to discuss your other request with my people," the old man says. "Our secrets are not easily bartered."

Sensei bows respectfully. "We must each do what we think is right. Only you can judge if any secret is worth more than Enlai's life."

"Wait here," the old man orders. As he rises, men rush to help, but he waves them away. Except Big Wu.

"He's not telling us all he knows," Taji whispers.

Even though we're alone, I feel like the walls are watching and listening.

Sensei feels it, too, and answers softly. "It does not matter. He is telling us what we need to know. No one needs to know everything."

He means me, too. I turn away, pretending I don't understand.

"But Elder Lin said he was willing to kill you," says Mikko.

"And if he was going to hide something, then he certainly would have hidden that," says Sensei. "I am willing to trust the Lin."

"Are you sure?" Yoshi asks.

"I am sure we need their help to rescue Kyoko,"

Sensei says. "I have looked down the path Lu Zeng has chosen. It is dark, but those who travel it grow strong and powerful."

"Surely evil is not more powerful than good?" says Taji.

Sensei shakes his head sadly. "An evil man will do things no other man dreams of, but do not worry. A good man never fights alone. He always has allies willing to aid him."

If it will help defeat Lu Zeng, then I'll trust the Lin, too.

See how easy it is? Sensei says.

Yes.

But it seems much harder to trust Yoshi. I expect the Lin to follow their own path, but Yoshi and I are blood brothers. We used to walk in each other's footsteps.

The old man returns, carrying a pot of ointment and a bundle of scrolls. "It is agreed," he says, unrolling a map.

But not everyone agrees. Big Wu stands glaring, muscled arms crossed tight.

"Rub this cream on your ankle." Elder Lin hands me the small pot. "You will only need to use it twice. This evening and again in the morning."

The ointment is cold and numbs my ankle. Cautiously, I lean on my foot. It's a miracle cure.

"Thank you," I murmur.

Elder Lin nods. He points to a place on the map. "Enlai and Kyoko are being held prisoners here in Secretary Lu Zeng's palace. The Temple of Scientific Excellence."

Sensei laughs, and Elder Lin joins in.

I don't get the joke, and my friends shake their heads too. Mikko pokes me, and I jab him back. We jostle Taji, who shoves back, bumping into Yoshi. We're not interested in maps and the eccentric humor of old men. We just want to rescue Kyoko. To brandish our swords and make Lu Zeng pay.

"Perhaps my restless students could begin their Lin training now," suggests Sensei.

Waving his hand, Elder Lin calls Big Wu over. "Take the samurai students into the center of the tunnels and teach them the basics of tracking."

"As you wish," the man grumbles.

We know another bear of a man, Sensei's old student, the famous swordsman Mitsuka Manuyoto. Mitsuka is the sort of bear who wraps his arms around you in a great friendly bear hug. This new bear would squeeze a man to death.

Big Wu leads us to another room, moving a cupboard to reveal an exit. "I do not think we should teach our ways to strangers. If it was up to me, I would leave you in the tunnels. The Lin don't need your help to rescue Enlai."

"We appreciate your honesty," Yoshi says. "But tonight we are your students, and we will respect you as our teacher even if you would rather be elsewhere. Our master would be disappointed if we did not."

Shrugging, the man climbs into the tunnel.

"He knows how to make a person feel nervous, doesn't he?" whispers Taji.

"It's all a strategy. Just like earlier," says Yoshi, stepping into the tunnel. "He wants us to feel afraid."

"We're not." Mikko follows next. "Samurai kids are not afraid of anything — not even grumpy forest people."

When we are all inside with the door closed, Big Wu produces four headbands. "These blindfolds will prevent you from using the shadows or pockets of gloom to mark our passage. Luckily, you have me; otherwise you would never find your way back out."

Maybe *I* wouldn't be able to, but I know Taji could. The Golden Bat doesn't need to see where he is going.

We follow quietly, listening hard for anything that might help. Suddenly, our new teacher stops.

"Here we will practice hiding and seeking. You must count to one hundred then call out, 'Finished.' Three times I will call 'I am here,' and then you must trace my voice to find me. It will not be easy in this tunnel, where sound plays tricks on the ears. Let us see what a samurai kid can do."

"One, two, three . . ." I begin counting.

"Thirty . . . forty . . ." Taji has a turn.

Yoshi's voice rumbles against the ceiling. "Seventy-five . . ."

"One hundred. Finished!" Mikko yells.

Clunk. The door closes. For the second time tonight, we're trapped in a tunnel.

CHAPTER SIX

礼

A LESSON
LEARNED

I tear off my headband. Slowly, my eyes adjust to the gloom. We're in a large hollow area, the center of six tunnels. One leads back to the room with Sensei, but what if the others end in piles of bones? It is said that the Lin can make people disappear. Perhaps this is how they do it.

"Do you think he's trying to get rid of us?" Mikko asks nervously.

Taji shakes his head. "He wouldn't dare disobey Elder Lin's instructions."

Phew. I breathe a sigh of relief.

"I think this is our first lesson," Taji continues. "He is testing to see if we can find our way to the tunnel entrance without help. When he thinks we're frightened enough, he'll return to rescue us. He's probably laughing about it now."

"I'd like to teach him a lesson," Yoshi growls.

"We can," I say. "Instead of trying to retrace the way we came, let's find another way out. Then he'll have to search for us."

"We'll be the ones laughing then." Mikko's eyes glisten with mischief. "But I don't want Sensei to worry that we are lost."

Taji smiles. "Sensei will know where we are."

Of course he will. Because I will tell him.

"Do you know which way to go?" Yoshi asks Taji.

Stepping inside each tunnel entrance, Taji breathes deep, smelling the air. "This is a dead end," he says at the first and second.

"We came in here." He points. "And Big Wu went out that way. He's probably waiting outside." Taji smiles. "But there's another exit behind Mikko. I can smell fresh air and ripe peaches."

"Then we'll go in that direction," decides Yoshi. "I'm feeling hungry."

Yoshi is our leader, and I'll follow him and his stomach to the tunnel's end, but I still can't walk beside him. Things have shifted for us. Yoshi is my friend, but he's not my brother anymore. I fall in step beside Mikko.

Beneath the earth, the air is damp and green. It smells like fallen leaves and things that grow on the forest floor. No wonder the Lin people use a tunnel system. It's a lot like their forest home.

Soon the aroma of peaches tempts all of our noses, but as we grow closer, the tunnel shrinks and grows darker until Yoshi has to crawl on his hands and knees and Mikko, Taji, and I are bent over like old willow trees.

"Are we nearly there?" I ask Taji.

Yoshi grunts as his shoulders scrape on the walls. If we don't find the way out soon, we'll have to turn back.

"Wait here," says Taji. "I am the thinnest, so I can squeeze through and check what lies ahead."

Yoshi starts to shake.

"What's wrong?" I ask.

"I can't breathe," he wheezes.

There is nothing wrong with the air. It tastes good, like mushrooms and new growth.

"Breathe slowly," Mikko says.

"I can't!" Yoshi is panicking. Gasping, arms flailing, he tries to rise. "I have to get out of here."

Dirt drops through cracks in the wooden ceiling. If Yoshi pushes too hard, the tunnel might collapse.

I wrap my arms around him, and Mikko does the same. It takes two of us to hold Yoshi tight and still. For the moment, his secret doesn't matter. My friend is in trouble.

"We're in a bend," Taji calls. "A few more steps and the tunnel widens."

"Did you hear that, Yoshi?" I say. "You'll be able to stand soon."

Yoshi edges forward, Mikko and I gently pushing from behind until we can feel Taji tugging, too.

We spill into a widened area with a rope ladder leading toward freedom.

Yoshi stands and stretches his feet and arms. He twists his neck back and forth until finally he is ready to lead us up the ladder. All we can do now is hope that he'll be able to lift the hatch to the outside when he reaches the top.

Just then, we hear Yoshi grunt and the cover to the tunnel opening. A shaft of moonlight reaches down to tap me on the shoulder. I stifle the urge to cheer. We don't know yet where the tunnel has led us. Taji climbs up next, followed by Mikko. I lash my crutch to my chest again and go last. I'm the slowest of all, pulling myself by my arms. Every time I rest my foot on the rung of the ladder, my ankle throbs and burns, but at least I can walk on it. By the time I reach the hatch and lift myself out, my friends are resting under the peach tree.

"About time," teases Mikko, his mouth full of fruit. "What kept you?"

"Here." Yoshi tosses a peach to me. "I saved the biggest, juiciest one for you. Do you want to sit beside me?" he asks, his voice full of hope.

But nothing has been resolved as far as I am concerned.

"Do you want to tell me where Mei and Du Feng are?" I reply.

He shakes his head. "I can't." He looks sad, but I'm not falling for that.

I push past him to sit beside Mikko and place Yoshi's peach on the ground.

"You're being silly, Niya. It's nothing personal. None of us know," Mikko whispers.

"It's not the same. You don't want to," I mutter.

Mikko prods me in the stomach. "Well, what if I had a secret?"

"Do you?" I ask.

"No."

"Good. I'll stay here then. You can have that peach if you like."

"Our new allies have strange ways," Yoshi says,

pretending he didn't hear my conversation with Mikko.

"It's not like being at the Owl Dojo. There we were among friends. The Lin only want to assist us so we can help them. I wonder what will happen if we can't rescue Enlai," Taji muses.

In the silence, we all wonder. It's probably not good.

The air is warm, and Yoshi removes his jacket, bundling it into a pillow to rest against. He yawns loudly. Mikko too.

But not me. I'm not sleepy. Nothing feels right. Kyoko might be in danger, and I can't even talk to Yoshi without getting angry.

"I think I'll go for a walk and stretch my leg," I say.

"I'll come with you." Taji rises, too. He can sense a change in my mood as easily as a shift in the wind.

"That's a good idea," Yoshi says. "No one should go wandering alone."

"I can look after myself," I snap. "You're not in charge of me."

Yoshi looks hurt but I ignore that, stomping into the darkness. Taji hurries behind me.

"It is his responsibility," he says quietly. "Sensei

expects Yoshi to look after us, and he would be upset with him if anything happened to you."

I sigh. "You're right. I get so frustrated that Yoshi won't tell me where Mei and Du Feng are."

"Why do you need to know?"

Taji's question makes me stop walking. I don't need to know. "I guess it's just because Yoshi knows."

Taji laughs. "You sound like a little boy, Niya."

I glare at Taji, but it's wasted. He can't see my face.

"Don't you trust Sensei?" he asks.

"Yes, of course," I say.

"Well then, perhaps there is a reason for you not to know."

Taji drapes his arm around my shoulder. He's grown taller than me, and I hadn't even noticed! "Being blind, I have to trust my friends all the time. Even when they make me cranky." He pauses. "Even when they act like spoiled children."

"If you weren't blind, I'd give you a huge shove to send you sprawling." I put my arm around him, too.

Taji just laughs again. "And I trust you won't."

"How come you can always see things so much clearer than me?" I ask.

"No distractions," Taji says. "You should try closing your eyes more often."

It's good advice. Maybe I will.

By the time we have circled back around to the peach tree, I feel much calmer. I sit next to Yoshi. It's hard to accept a secret between friends, but I'm going to keep trying.

It's even harder to sit here knowing that Kyoko might need us. But there's nothing I can do to help her tonight, except hope. Mikko yawns, and one by one we feel his lethargy wrap us in its cloak. Taji yawns. Yoshi too. Finally, I yawn loudest of all.

I'm so tired. Overhead the passing night stars flicker and blink, counting the space between sleeping and waking. Bats wheel and screak. As I watch, one of the bats grows larger and blacker.

I close my eyes to find that Taji is right. It's much easier to think like this. I imagine Sensei flying with the bats.

"I knew I'd find you eventually!" Big Wu bellows.

Around me, my friends stir. We wait for the lecture to follow, but instead, Big Wu laughs.

"Boys will be boys," he says, wedging himself between Mikko and me.

There's not enough room. We're packed like sushi rolls in a rice-paper box. Too tight. So I poke Taji until he wriggles over.

"You're not angry?" Yoshi asks. "I thought you didn't like us."

"I, too, have learned a lesson. My judgment was hasty. Now I am pleased to have such clever students." He stretches and scratches his nose. "I hear you already know the Flying Locust Attack. Good. I will not have to teach you that, either."

"We don't know any Locust Attack," Mikko admits. "But we are willing to learn."

Big Wu laughs.

"You know it all right, and Yen-Fu has a lump on his head to prove it. In fact, many of his scouts have sore heads. Your stone-throwing is very accurate." He laughs again. "You remind me of my sons. I have four boys, and I am used to such tricks."

"Have they returned to the forest?" Taji asks.

"Yes. Our people are leaving Beijing forever. Elder Lin says the city will soon fall to invaders. Maybe not today, not tomorrow, but before the year is ended. We would all be gone now except we cannot leave Enlai behind."

"Don't worry. Sensei will rescue Enlai and Kyoko." Yoshi's voice is strong and sure. I wish I felt like that, too.

Big Wu smiles. "I have a daughter, too. She is more trouble than all my boys together."

"It's the same with Kyoko," agrees Mikko.

The silence fills with our fear and drops to sit heavy on my chest. "Look, there's the *tsuzumi* drum." Yoshi points into the sky to where the stars form the corners of an hourglass shape.

"And the kimono sleeve. And the *shakuhachi*," says Mikko.

"It's like Kyoko is with us. Maybe it's a good sign," I say. And when I concentrate hard, I imagine I can hear the sound of her bamboo flute.

"I'm sure it is," says Taji. "I wish I could see the stars, too."

"I will tell you a story about the stars. What you cannot see, you can hear and imagine," Big Wu promises. "Then we will practice."

"Now? It's nighttime!" says Mikko, suddenly paying attention.

"You cannot waste all night sleeping if you are to learn the ways of the forest demons." Big Wu contorts his face in mock fear. "Night is when the demons come out to play and terrorize passersby."

"All right," Mikko agrees begrudgingly. "Story first."

"This is the story of the Dipper Mother, a great queen of the Dragon Throne, who promised that her children would protect and care for the earth. One day, she went to bathe in a pool. The fish of good fortune swam around her, and seven lotus buds rose from the mud on the bottom of the pond. Each bud opened to reveal a star. See those seven stars? They are the children of the Dipper Mother, keeping an eye on the world below. And if you cannot see them in the sky, close your eyes tight, and you will find them imprinted on your eyelids."

I try, and it's true.

"In Japan, we call them the Seven Brothers," Yoshi

says. "We say they climbed up to the sky and changed into stars to escape a monster *oni*."

There are many ways of looking at things, Sensei teaches.

"Do you think one thing can change into another like that, like the lotus and the brothers?" asks Mikko.

"Maybe." Big Wu smiles. "My daughter shines like a star, not at all dull like me. Perhaps she came from a flower."

In that case, maybe Kyoko did as well.

"Tell him about the *tengu*," says Mikko, digging me in the ribs.

I shake my head.

"Some people say our teacher is a mountain demon who transforms into a great bat-bird and flies across the moon," Taji says. "Even Elder Lin knows the story."

"Anything is possible," Big Wu says, scratching his behind.

Sensei says that, too. All the time.

A large bat flies across the sky, silhouetted against the moon.

"It was just a bat," I say, kicking Mikko before he says anything more.

"In China, a bat is a sign of good fortune," says Big Wu.

"In Japan, it is sometimes a sign of an overactive imagination." I poke Mikko with my toe.

Plop.

We all jump.

"I need to resume my teaching urgently, especially if you are afraid of this." Big Wu picks up the fallen peach.

"I am not afraid of fruit," Mikko says, jumping up. "My sword could make salad of that in three slices."

"Shh!" Big Wu pulls him to the ground with a thump. "City street patrol." He points to a soldier emerging from the gloom to pass the door of the courtyard.

"You almost made salad out of us, Mikko," says Yoshi.

"*Hmph.* I could easily fight two of the Emperor's soldiers," Mikko boasts.

"I should think so," says Big Wu. "I am wasting my time if you cannot. The Emperor's soldiers sneak like water buffalo and move like turtles. Come with me." He rises. "Tonight I will teach you about shadows. The Lin are the shadow people. We move in and out of the changing light. That is what makes us so difficult to see."

Any tactic that could hide Big Wu is worth knowing.

We follow him into the alley, darting between the shadows to briefly rest in the darkest spots, before moving again.

"This is easy," Mikko says, gloating.

"You think so?" our teacher asks.

"Yes." I agree with Mikko.

Tu-wheet. Big Wu whistles into the darkness. "Over here," he calls to the soldier. "Test time," he whispers, then fades into the night.

There's no time to talk or discuss a plan of action. The soldier has already turned toward us.

Yoshi heads for the camouflage of the courtyard wall. Taji climbs into the branches of the nearest tree, and Mikko scuttles away. I take a step, the way Big Wu taught, moving from one shadow into the next. Always moving. The soldier looks directly into my eyes. Even if he can't see me, surely he can hear the sound of my heart. *Thump. Thump.*

"No one here," the soldier mutters as he turns away.

"Ten hours is too long for one patrol shift. Now I am seeing things."

The stars wink. My heart beats like a *tsuzumi* drum, and my sigh of relief whistles like a *shakuhachi* flute. Leaves rustle as Taji slides to the ground beside me.

From nowhere, Big Wu materializes. "That was fun, wasn't it?"

"It was," I admit. "When I wasn't scared to death."

"How did you know we would escape the soldier?" Yoshi asks.

"You would not even have to hide to do that," Big Wu says. "Now, let's pick some peaches, and I will take you to your sleeping quarters. Your master is waiting there."

I bet he's already asleep.

I heard that, Sensei whispers.

Then he yawns.

I heard that. Sleep well, Master.

"Tomorrow you will have a new teacher." Big Wu grins.

"Who?" Mikko asks.

"Jang the Poisoner," says Big Wu. "It would not be a good idea to play tricks on him."

The soldier looks directly into my eyes.

"Doesn't he have any children we would remind him of?" Taji asks.

"They say he got rid of them. And the Poisoner would know how."

In the shadows, we can't tell whether Big Wu is serious or not.

CHAPTER SEVEN

勇

THE POISONER

"We must not keep Master Jang waiting." Sensei strides ahead.

"But what about Kyoko?" Taji asks. "Why does she have to wait?"

"We must plan carefully. Lu Zeng is no ordinary opponent, and we will need Master Jang's help in the days to follow," says Sensei.

Jang the Poisoner.

His name sends icy shivers down my spine. I can see him in my imagination: a huge man in dark robes, towering over us. Yellow teeth. A cavernous mouth. This is a man who holds death between stained fingers. Even one as evil as Lu Zeng comes to him for advice.

"I don't know why we have to have more lessons," Mikko says with a groan. "I don't need to poison anyone. All I need is my sword."

Sensei shrugs. "It is good to know many skills. Is there such a thing as too much learning?"

"Yes," Yoshi, Mikko, and Taji chorus.

But for once, I don't mind. I'd do anything to set Kyoko free, and if we need to learn more skills, I'll make sure I'm at the top of the class.

"Sometimes a little poison is a useful drug. You

already know it is much easier to outwit a sleeping opponent," says Sensei.

"But why do we need to learn how to use potions when you can teach us to knock them out with a finger to their necks?" I ask.

"I wish it was that easy," Sensei replies. "But that is the one thing I cannot teach you. Nor can I promise you will ever learn it. You cannot teach the heart to beat or the eye to blink or a finger to absorb another's *ki*. Some things simply happen."

I hope it happens for me.

Sensei knocks, and the door opens to reveal a little brown man in a dirty white shirt. His nose is big and out of place. He's so short, he doesn't even reach up to my shoulder, but he easily stares us down. He has a gaze strong enough to make even Yoshi hunch his shoulders. The Poisoner might be small in stature, but he radiates great power.

"Good morning, Master Jang." Sensei bows.

"Welcome, welcome." There is nothing frightening about Master Jang when he smiles. His face creases from one side to the other.

"Do you like to cook, boys?" he asks.

"I like to eat," volunteers Yoshi.

The Poisoner laughs. "I would suggest you be careful what you taste here today. The wrong bowl will give you serious stomach pain. Come with me, and I'll teach you how to make a meal you wouldn't wish on your worst enemy."

In the kitchen, a row of blue bowls stretches across the bench.

The Poisoner taps his face. "See this nose?"

We nod politely. It's impossible to miss.

"A poisoner's greatest assets are his sense of smell and his knowledge of plants and minerals. A good sniff can sometimes tell you when there is poison in the air or on your plate." He taps Taji on the nose. "You have a special advantage. A good poisoner disguises his work well, and those who depend on their sight are easy targets."

"Close your eyes," he says, handing me a bowl. "What can you smell?"

I take a sniff. Peach blossoms. That can't be right. I take another sniff.

"Believe in your nose, boy," Master Jang says. "What did the first sniff say?"

It's always hard to trust. "I smell peaches."

"That's right. The pit in the middle of the peach is poisonous."

"But we eat peaches all the time. We had lots last night," says Taji. "They didn't even give us a bellyache."

"And how many pits did you swallow?" Master Jang asks.

"None," Mikko says.

"Even then, you would have to eat hundreds of peach pits before you felt ill. But when I grind them up, I can put enough powder in a bowl of porridge to make breakfast the last meal of the day."

"I thought the peach tree was a symbol of long life, and that's why Chinese gardens are full of them," says Yoshi.

Master Jang laughs. "I plant my peach trees so that my enemy will not have a life at all."

He takes the long dagger from his belt and lays it on the table. The blade gleams, bright and murderous. It doesn't have the beauty of a samurai sword, and it can't sing a single note. But no man would want to argue with it in the dark *hutong* alleys of the Forbidden City.

"Poison is like a sword," Master Jang says. "It has two sharp edges. One that can take life away and one that can give it back. Poison can be medicine or can cause a painful death. Sometimes the only difference is in the size of the serving. Come."

He snaps his fingers, and we follow him into a smaller room. In the center is a large table with red and blue bowls and a vase containing small purple flowers. It wouldn't score many points in the ikebana competition at the annual Samurai Trainee Games. A samurai must find beauty in the arc of his sword and in the arranging of flowers. But a poisoner has different priorities.

"Here." Master Jang offers a flower to Mikko.

Uncertain, Mikko shakes his head.

"The flower won't hurt you, but the soup I make from its stems will give you a killer stomachache." Master Jang laughs. "Have a smell."

We pass the flower around.

"Yuck!" Mikko sputters.

"Disgusting," Yoshi says with a snort.

Even Sensei holds his nose.

It smells like the dead bird I found behind the *ryu* storehouse. Stomach heaving, I hand the flower back to Master Jang.

"It's called aconite. Such a pretty blossom," he says.

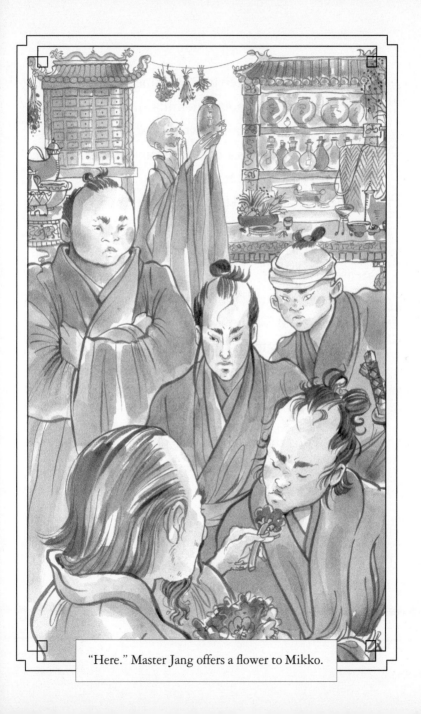

"Here." Master Jang offers a flower to Mikko.

"But looks can be deceiving. One smear of aconite soup on an arrowhead is enough to kill. Chinese assassins use aconite to make a Plum Flower Sleeve Arrow. Watch."

Master Jang takes a cylinder from the shelf and fits five small arrows into it.

"See this string?" He tugs and the arrows fly out to embed themselves deep in the wooden bench.

"A very effective weapon to have up your sleeve," Sensei says.

Master Jang nods. "First, you will feel the tingling. Numbing cold. Clammy skin. Fading pulse. Then you'll gasp and struggle for breath until everything in your body stops dead. There is no cure for the right dose."

My stomach is feeling even worse now, but Master Jang is having fun.

"Now for the other edge of the sword. A pinch of aconite makes a sweet tea perfect for aches and pains from your head to your big toe. Try some." He gestures to the red bowls.

No one steps forward.

"You can trust me, boys," Master Jang says.

I look at Sensei, who nods.

It is time to practice trusting, he says.

Cautiously, I take a small sip. "It's really good," I say, passing the bowl to Mikko.

Master Jang removes a pouch from inside his jacket and empties white powder from it into a blue bowl. "In my kitchen, red bowls are for food, but a blue bowl should never touch your lips," he says.

Taji sniffs the blue bowl and shakes his head. "I can't smell anything."

"Arsenic is a very useful poison. No taste and no smell. Some assassins mix it with sand and fling it in an enemy's eyes. But you and I know that blinding a man doesn't disable him." He smiles at Taji. "I prefer to know the assignment has been completed. A big dose for a violent death or a small dose over a long time for a slow weakening of the body. Arsenic is easily dissolved in food or water."

"I believe an emperor once had it served to him smeared on bread," says Sensei.

"Peach jam would definitely have been safer." Master Jang rubs his hands together.

His eyes bright, it's easy to see that the Poisoner loves his work. I shudder. I don't think I ever want to eat or drink again.

"Ho! Jang!"

The familiar voice of Big Wu calls through the house, soon followed by the man himself. He stoops into the doorway. In his arms is the boy we met in the street yesterday.

"This young one had a little trouble with the law. He stuck his hand in where he shouldn't have."

It's obvious from the expression on Big Wu's face that he thoroughly approves of our pickpocket friend.

"What's your name, boy?" asks Master Jang.

The boy looks frightened, but Big Wu smiles encouragingly at him.

"Chen," he mutters. "A soldier slashed my arm."

Fist clenched, he grimaces as Master Jang inspects the damage. "The wound will need sewing together. You are lucky the soldier did not slice your arm off."

"Lately, everyone is telling me how lucky I am." Chen grins weakly at Sensei.

"And you are also lucky to be here. Even the Emperor does not have a doctor as skilled as me. But first, there is the matter of payment. Perhaps you have something to trade for my services?"

What could a street boy have that Master Jang would want? It hardly seems fair to ask.

"What about your boots?" Master Jang suggests.

Chen nods.

"It is a matter of honor," Sensei explains softly to us. "The Lin do not work for nothing. A payment must be made."

A samurai can understand that. But we temper honor with other things. *Chi, jin, yu.* Wisdom, benevolence, and courage. The way of the warrior. We don't seek honor by taking the shoes from the feet of a poor street kid.

It's not right, I say.

Sensei grins. *What does the boy do for a living?*

Slowly, I grin, too, because now I understand. Chen can easily steal another pair of shoes as long as he has a good arm to do it with.

Master Jang takes a strip of green ribbon from his pocket and drapes it around his neck. The Poisoner is now a healer. The other edge of the sword.

He removes the flowers and bowls from the table. Gently, Big Wu lifts Chen onto it.

Chen clamps his teeth shut and closes his eyes, trying to shut out the pain.

"After the first two needles are inserted, you will not feel anything," promises Master Jang.

"May I have a closer look?" Sensei asks. "Acupuncture is practiced in Japan, but I have not seen it performed. I would be honored to learn from you, Master."

"Please." The Poisoner beckons to Sensei.

Now I can't see much at all. Maybe that's a good thing.

"Some say acupuncture began hundreds of years ago, when an imperial soldier was hit by an arrow and noticed that it relieved the pain in other parts of his body," Master Jang explains.

"I'm not surprised. If I got an arrow in my back, I bet I'd forget about the one in my leg," whispers Yoshi.

Master Jang takes three needles from a bowl. "This will be enough."

"It is a very deep cut," notes Sensei.

Chen leans forward to look, too. It's not a good move. His eyes roll back, and he flops down like one of my sister Ayame's rag dolls. If he's lucky, he'll sleep through the rest of the operation.

"This powder will help. It is excellent for open wounds." Master Jang sprinkles a fine brown dust into the gaping wound.

"Ah, ground tortoiseshell." Sensei approves.

"The best. From Secretary Lu Zeng's own supplies."

"He gave it to you?" Taji asks.

"Secretary Lu Zeng does not like to pay his bills, so I collected the payment myself. He will not miss it. He has tanks full of tortoises and more shells than any man would need to cure a lifetime of patients."

"Why does he collect tortoise shells?" asks Yoshi.

Master Jang laughs. "The Secretary thinks he can read secrets in the patterns of the shells. 'Oracle dragon bones,' he calls them. That man is so desperate to learn the secret of long life, he would even ask a tortoise."

"A man who has no respect for the lives of others does not deserve even one extra day," I mutter through clenched teeth.

"I would like to end his life today," Mikko says.

"The skills I teach you will help your battle against Secretary Lu Zeng and others like him," Master Jang promises. "No man can live forever."

"If Lu Zeng wants to know how to grow old, he should ask a Zen master. He should ask me," says Sensei.

It's a good point. Sensei is the oldest person I have

met. His face is lined and wrinkled like crushed rice paper. Some people say he is over a hundred years old.

"What is the secret to long life?" I ask. Sensei has many secrets, and I would gladly learn this one first.

"NOTHING." Sensei laughs.

In Zen, NOTHING is most important. NOTHING is more important than living forever. It's a joke Lu Zeng would never understand. His weakness gives me hope. Soon we will rescue Kyoko and Enlai, and, in Master Jang's care, Chen will eventually recover. Master Jang takes out a spool of thread from a nearby drawer.

"Allow me to help," offers Sensei. "I have had years of practice. Samurai kids are not always careful with their swords."

With small stitches, our teacher closes the gash. Then Master Jang removes the needles.

Chen wakes with a start, his brow creased in pain. "Aaaargh," he moans softly.

"Here, drink this." The Poisoner tips a bamboo flask to the boy's lips.

Chen gags and sputters.

"Your next meal will taste better," says Master Jang.

"I can brew more than a poisoner's potion. I am a good cook, too."

"Excellent," Sensei says, rubbing his belly. "My students have been tested by your people, and now I think I will test your claim."

Master Jang nods. "It is only fair. I must provide something as payment for your help."

"Then perhaps I have also earned those shoes," Sensei says, gesturing to Chen's boots.

"I think you have," agrees Master Jang.

Sensei measures the shoes against his long skinny feet. "They will not fit me, so I will gift them to someone whose feet are the right size," he says, returning them to Chen.

"Thank you," the boy whispers to Sensei. "I owe you my life and my shoes."

"But I did the acupuncture, so perhaps I deserve one boot," suggests Jang with a sly smile.

"You are right," says Sensei, "but I have already given those boots away. Allow me to offer one of my sandals."

Master Jang takes the sandal, holding it against his small foot. "It appears your foot is much larger than mine. Thank you for the offer, but I will return your sandal."

Together they laugh.

"What was all that about?" Mikko whispers.

"Lin honor," I remind him. As long as payment is made, it does not matter if you have anything in your hand when the deal is done.

"This will help you rest and recover." Master Jang gives Chen another drink.

It works fast. *Zzzz. Zzzz.* The room fills with the sound of Chen's snoring.

"He'll be all right, won't he?" asks Taji.

"Of course. He has the best doctors in all of China and Japan," says Master Jang. "Now I have a present for my worthy assistant."

From a narrow drawer, Master Jang removes a long, thin sword.

"This is a *wodao.* The Emperor's armory master says it is an improvement on the samurai sword. I doubt that, but it is still a fine piece of workmanship."

Sensei's eyes gleam more brightly than the blade does as he takes the offered gift. No samurai can resist a well-crafted sword.

Our teacher bows. "I am in your debt."

I suspect that Master Jang likes it that way. But Sensei is not worried, so neither am I. He tucks the *wodao* into his sash.

"While Chen sleeps, we have lunch to eat and more lessons to learn." Master Jang waves us toward the first room.

Lunch is a tray of steamed dumplings filled with sweet and sour surprises. All of them taste and smell good. The Poisoner *is* a wonderful cook. The afternoon passes quickly, and then, with one last look at Chen, still snoring, it's time to go.

"Niya." Master Jang calls me aside. "I have a final medicine to administer." He hands me a peach pit.

"What's it for?" I ask.

"It is for what ails you. Put it in your pocket to remind you that poison is much safer inside your jacket than inside your heart. A warrior must keep his mind as healthy as his body."

I want to say I don't know what he is talking about, but I do. I haven't spoken to Yoshi at all today. "Thank you," I say, my hands closing around the stone. "I'll try harder."

"Good-bye, good-bye." Master Jang ushers us out the door, eager to get back to his concoctions and powders. "We will meet again. Soon, I think."

The White Crane has very sharp eyes, and in that last moment before the door closes, I see Master Jang give Sensei a peach pit, too.

CHAPTER EIGHT

真

FORBIDDEN CITY

Rap-tap. Rap-tap-tap.

Only the Lin know we are in this house, and we're not expecting them this morning. Sensei lifts his finger, and Mikko moves to the door, sword in hand.

"What's the password?" Yoshi asks.

"San," replies a voice.

It's the Chinese word for umbrella. Elder Lin chose it because he says soon the sky will fill with dragon's-breath clouds, and then it will rain.

"I'll need an umbrella, too," the voice continues, "if I am to be met by another shower of lotus stones."

Sensei laughs, and Yoshi opens the door to Yen-Fu, the man we first met in the marketplace.

"I bring news from Elder Lin. Secretary Lu Zeng is performing an important ceremony this afternoon. To ensure that the Imperial Troops have good fortune in the battles to come."

"Is there going to be a war?" asks Yoshi.

"There is always a war somewhere." Sensei clicks his tongue in disapproval.

But Yen-Fu grins, his eyes bright with the hope that soon the Emperor will have fewer soldiers. "The farmers and peasants are rebelling. There is much wealth inside

Beijing, but outside, even rice grains are sometimes hard to find. Messengers say that the threat from the North grows stronger, too. I have heard whispers that we are not winning and that soon the raiders will cross the Great Wall."

"The core of the city is decaying, and Lu Zeng is a part of that. Like a rotten plum, Beijing will fall," says Sensei.

"I would not like to be in the Emperor's slippers when that happens." Yen-Fu smirks.

There is a harshness to the Lin that makes me shudder. I would trust them with my life, as long as I had made a deal beforehand. But I would never trust them with my samurai heart.

"Anyway," says Yen-Fu, "by then my people will have returned to the forest where our families are already waiting."

"The Emperor might need your services," protests Mikko.

Yen-Fu smiles. "But I will not need his. I will be gone."

It's all about striking a good deal, and, despite his wealth, the Dragon Emperor has nothing the Lin would value in a trade. Except Enlai. But we will have returned him to his grandfather long before the walls are breached.

"Where will Lu Zeng be performing the ceremony?" asks Sensei.

"In the great square in front of the Hall of Supreme Harmony. Do you know the way?"

Sensei nods. "Yes. Thank you."

"Then I will leave you to your plans. I have many of my own to make. Elder Lin has said we will be gone by the end of the week."

Sensei nods again. He got the message. He is expected to rescue Enlai before the deadline.

Or else . . . what?

I would not like to make Elder Lin angry.

Sensei is not concerned, humming to himself as he takes Lu Zeng's scroll message from his pocket. "We will go to the Imperial Ceremony. It is where the Twelve Symbols of Sovereignty can be found, and we already have an invitation," he says. "It is time for Lu Zeng to answer for his actions. It is time to set Kyoko free."

"It might be a trap," warns Yoshi.

"I am sure it is." Sensei grins. "But if I am trapped

with Lu Zeng, then he is also caught with me. I will have him exactly where I need him. I am not worried."

But the White Crane is. Lu Zeng is a powerful opponent, and he has had many years to wait and prepare. Sensei is a master swordsman, skilled with *bo* and blade, but he is tired from many months of travel. The battle ahead will not be easy. How do you cut a path through darkness? How do you wound a man without a soul?

Tucking the scroll back into his pocket, Sensei rises to his feet. "By afternoon, we will be inside the Forbidden City."

We're nervous and fearful, but most of all, we're determined to rescue Kyoko.

On the long walk down the central street, it begins to rain.

"Dragon tears," Sensei says. "But they will not be enough to wash Beijing clean."

The red walls tower above us, and above them I see yellow-gold roofs. Ordinary people are not allowed inside. The penalty is death.

"We must use the far-eastern entrance," Sensei instructs. "Only the Emperor can pass through the center of the Great Gate of the Forbidden City. When I was awarded first place in the Imperial Examinations, I was carried in a sedan chair through the Emperor's Archway, with Lu Zeng riding behind me."

In China they do not value the sanctity of a sword, but they place a lot of value on the footpath to the Forbidden City. One step in the wrong place and you're dead.

I hope Sensei was right about his invitation.

At the Great Gate, we are met by the familiar voice of the soldier from the Outer City Gate.

"Let them through," he says. "This man is Jin Shi Ki-Yaga, a great teacher from Japan and the personal guest of no less than the Esteemed Secretary of the Board of Rites."

Waving our thanks, we pass under the great arch and into the heart of the Middle Kingdom.

A throng of people gathers for the afternoon ceremony. Army officers, haughty and confident. Administrator mandarins with their badge of rank proudly displayed.

"Where is your badge, Sensei?" Mikko asks.

Our master taps his traveling staff on the ground.

"Hidden away. If someone saw it, I might be called upon to make a list." Sensei sighs. "There are always lists and inventories here. After my examination, the top candidates were given the task of writing down all the treasures in the Forbidden City palaces. One hundred scholars, including Lu Zeng and me, worked for over a month."

"I can't imagine anything more boring," says Mikko.

Yoshi grins. "I can't imagine that much treasure."

"Even now someone is listing everyone who passes through the Forbidden City gates," says Sensei. "Lu Zeng will already know we are here."

I imagine his cold black eyes boring through me.

But we are not quite there yet. In front of us, five bridges cross a river. Everyone is moving along the same path. I like to be different, so I hop toward the middle one.

"No, Niya," Sensei calls me back. "Only the Emperor may travel the middle path."

Taji laughs. "What would Buddha say?"

Buddha encourages the Middle Way. In Buddha's teachings, the middle path is meant for everyone, not just the Emperor. Even my one foot is welcome. But we are not making a point today, and the Forbidden City is the Emperor's home. If he wants a private footpath, then even Buddha cannot argue with that.

Patiently, we join the line to cross the bridge on the far left. Stone dragons and phoenixes watch us pass. No one else seems to notice.

"Lu Zeng will inspire our commanders to great deeds. They will crush the peasants like beetles in the dust," a mandarin scholar gloats, adjusting his black scholar's hat.

I shiver. A cockroach is just like a beetle, and most of the peasants we've met on our journey were kind and welcoming. I would raise my sword, too, if I didn't have enough to eat because the Emperor's men collected my crops as taxes. The Emperor's table is already full enough.

"We will never get there," grumbles another mandarin. "Every administrator and his dog is here today."

That's not quite true. There are no dogs. Except for the bats at night, a few pale goldfish in ponds, and stone guardians on the building roofs, I haven't seen any animals in Beijing.

Under the bridge, the water is crystal clear. Yellow-gold carp skim over the white tiles. No one stops to fish along the riverbank. Like so many other things in the Forbidden City, the river is a treasure made by man. Just for looking at. Only the Dragon Emperor may own fish of gold, and no man, no matter how hungry, would dare eat one of those.

We file through another gate and into an enormous courtyard. At the far end, a huge building sits on top of three gleaming white terraces. It leers like an open mouth, ready to swallow us whole. The Hall of Supreme Harmony. The place where Lu Zeng is waiting.

Maybe Kyoko is with him. I start to hop faster.

"What's the hurry?" Yoshi asks.

I wrap my fingers around the peach pit in my pocket.

"Kyoko might be with Lu Zeng," I say.

That makes us all walk faster. Even Sensei.

The rain has stopped, leaving the air muggy and uncomfortable.

"It's hot," Mikko complains, wiping the sweat from his headband.

There is not a shade tree to be seen in the Forbidden

City. Nothing is allowed to grow taller than the Son of Heaven's buildings. That's all right for him. He rides in a palanquin with a servant to fan his face. He doesn't have to walk anywhere he doesn't want to. And he never has to sit in the sun.

Already, a great ocean of people fills the square. It swells larger with every passing minute.

"How will Lu Zeng find us in this crowd?" asks Taji. You don't need sight to count the people; you only have to listen to the noise to know. It's like a flock of bats fighting. Thousands of them.

"Lu Zeng will see us," Sensei assures us.

Edging through the thickening throng, we move toward the front. If anyone stands in our way, Sensei shows the jade seal, and begrudgingly, they allow us through.

When we find a place to sit and wait, yet again I move as far away from Yoshi as possible.

"Why can't you make peace with Yoshi?" Mikko says. "You hardly speak to him anymore."

"He's very upset," adds Taji.

I look at Yoshi sitting on the other side of Sensei. "He knows how to fix things," I say.

"I thought you were the smart one, Niya," chides Taji. "You can't always know everything. Remember, you should trust your friends."

I look away.

"You have to talk to Yoshi," insists Mikko.

"Who's going to make me?" I retort.

Mikko's hand moves to his sword hilt.

Sensei raises his traveling staff just a little. Enough to remind us how it feels to be rapped around the ears with it.

I am disappointed, my master says. His words bat my ears just as harshly as any whack from his stick.

I am sorry, Sensei. I will try harder. I look at Yoshi and smile. He smiles back, a huge grin.

Now I am pleased, says Sensei.

"What can you see?" Taji asks, eager to know details.

"At the end of each of the tiers to the Hall is a great bronze vat of water. In case of fire. All the buildings here are made of wood," says Sensei.

Maybe that's where all the trees went.

"The tiers are decorated with urns," our teacher continues. "One for each of the Chinese provinces."

"And one for Lu Zeng." Mikko points to a tortoise-shaped urn.

"And one for Niya," adds Yoshi, laughing.

A majestic crane sculpture towers over the tortoise. Here the crane is the prince of feathers, the chosen one of souls on their way to Heaven. The White Crane likes that.

In the center of the lowest tier is a table covered in yellow-gold cloth, the Emperor's banners flying from poles on either side. Around us, voices rise and fall like chattering birds.

Boom. Boom. Boom.

The drums pound across the courtyard, and the flock is silent. Dead silent. Thousands of people have lost their voices in awe.

I don't want to look. I don't want to see the man who holds Kyoko imprisoned. The image in my mind is already frightening enough.

From the southern entrance to the Hall, lesser court officials file out to take their places on the lowest tier. Senior ministers flank each side of the middle level.

Ta-ra. Ta-ra.

A trumpet calls our attention to a man emerging on the highest step. His robe is bloodred, and the gold bands on his arms and ankles flash. It's like looking into the sun, and it makes my eyes hurt.

"That," Sensei whispers, "is Lu Zeng."

As Lu Zeng raises his arms, the crowd hushes from silence to something even deeper. Reverence and fear. Then the drums beat again.

Slowly.

Boom.

Ominously.

Boom.

Deafeningly.

Boom.

Lu Zeng drops his arms, and the world stops turning. The square is packed with thousands of officials, army lieutenants, and troop commanders. And every one of them is motionless. I'm afraid to breathe.

Into the silence, Sensei sneezes. Lu Zeng looks straight at him and smiles. It's the most terrifying sight so far.

"Welcome." Lu Zeng's voice is rich and warm. It

reaches out like the finest of gossamer nets, trapping us all. "Let us raise our voices to praise our emperor."

The crowd erupts in a cheer. "Hurrah! Hurrah! Long live the Emperor."

Trumpets sound and the silence returns.

"I, Secretary Lu Zeng, humble servant of the Dragon Throne, speak to you today on behalf of our emperor. Son of Heaven. Lord of Ten Thousand Years. Divine Ruler of the Middle Kingdom. Great and Celestial Dragon. Descendant of the Purple Pole Star . . ."

On and on he drones. No one has more names than the Emperor of China.

Finally, cymbals clash and drums roll. The crowd cheers again.

"Luckily, the Emperor has better things to do than listen to a roll call of his names. Imagine the noise if he was here," Taji whispers.

"The Son of Heaven has spent many hours in prayer beseeching his father, the King above, to guide our Dragon Armies to victory. Today I tell you the piety of the Son has been rewarded, and"—Lu Zeng's voice rises, and I can feel the net tighten—"we . . . will . . . be victorious!"

The square echoes with the stomp of boots. *"The*

Emperor! The Emperor!" the crowd roars. *"Secretary Lu Zeng!"*

When the noise subsides, Lu Zeng speaks again. "Our enemies will fall. We will triumph over the Mongol horsemen in the North; we will march over the rebel forces in the West; and we will raze the fields of the dissidents in the South. Already the fires burn."

"Foolish strategy. To set fire to one's own country," mutters Sensei.

"What sort of Emperor has to fight his own people, anyway?" asks Yoshi.

"One who has not been paying enough attention to his work," Sensei says.

"But he is the Son of Heaven," argues Mikko.

"All fathers have good sons and bad," replies Sensei. "Even the King of Heaven."

"Shh! If you are caught speaking, you will be punished severely," a man whispers. "You might be killed."

Even Mikko doesn't argue with that.

"The Twelve Symbols of Sovereignty bear witness," Lu Zeng intones.

One by one the attendants hold up the flags bearing the symbols.

"I, Lu Zeng, humble Secretary of the Board of Rites and your faithful servant, have also prayed for days to keep our people safe."

"Secretary Lu Zeng," the crowd bellows. *"Yah! Yah!"*

Sensei yawns. Lu Zeng couldn't possibly have heard, but he turns to look in our direction. It's a gaze that could set fire to fields without the need for any army.

"Come forward, General Chou," Lu Zeng commands.

A man steps from the front row, kneels before Lu Zeng, and presses his head to the ground. An attendant offers a bowl. Lu Zeng dips his fingers and touches them to the general's forehead.

"You will bring honor to the Middle Kingdom."

On cue, the crowd cheers.

Generals. Commanders. Lieutenants. There are hundreds of them. Each time, the act of anointment is repeated. Each time, the crowd cheers.

At last, it is over. Like a herd released, the square is a human stampede. We form a protective circle around our master.

"Jin Shi Ki-Yaga," says the thin voice of a bureaucrat who has snuck up behind us. "The Esteemed Secretary requests your presence."

"The Twelve Symbols of Sovereignty bear witness," Lu Zeng intones.

The mandarin is young and ambitious. His eyes glow with pride to serve such a man as Lu Zeng. "This way." He leads us onto the first tier and into a side room where his master is waiting.

Robes of red and rings of gold cannot hide a black heart. I can see it glittering through Lu Zeng's eyes as his gaze impales us each in turn.

"So you have found me, old friend." But there is no friendliness in Lu Zeng's greeting.

"You are not hard to find. You are an important official now," says Sensei. His voice is polite, but I hear the disdain in his words.

"People cower at the mention of my name, and I command great respect. Even the Emperor listens to me," Lu Zeng boasts.

But we don't.

"Where is Kyoko?" interrupts Taji.

"I see you have not taught your students any manners, Ki-Yaga."

"My student is making a good point. As any swordsman knows, a good point sinks deepest. Perhaps you have not been attending to your duties as you should.

Perhaps you have been wasting time on personal revenge instead," says Sensei.

Lu Zeng smirks. "I can see where your student gets his manners."

"I am one student short, and I have come to claim her." Sensei raps his staff on the tiled floor. "I have played your game, and now I am here."

"So you are, but you have not yet won. You see, I cannot give her to you, after all. You have come all this way for nothing."

Lu Zeng spins his thread of words, and I can feel the spiderweb noose tightening around our necks. "The girl is dead."

CHAPTER NINE

仁

LU ZENG'S LAIR

Like a spider, Lu Zeng watches his prey wriggle. My fear shakes his web, calling the darkness closer. He looks directly at me. Sneering.

Do not believe him, Sensei says.

I don't want to. But I'm scared that he might be telling the truth.

Sensei shakes his head, disappointed. *You will not trust Yoshi, who is like your brother, yet you would trust this man who stole Kyoko from us?*

Sensei's words help me untangle myself from the stories Lu Zeng spins.

"I don't believe it," I blurt out.

Lu Zeng's eyes narrow. "Why not?"

"Because Kyoko is much too useful," Sensei answers for me. "Especially to someone who wants to live forever."

"Ah, my old friend. Your mind is as sharp as always."

He doesn't know how sharp. If Sensei wanted, he could have a sword sticking out of Lu Zeng's back by now. Sensei is not Lu Zeng's friend.

"You are right, of course." Lu Zeng continues. "Kyoko is a gifted weaver and needleworker. That's why she must stay here. I cannot give up her clever fingers."

Kyoko can't even sew two sides of a rice bag together. Even Taji can do that, and he can't see either the cloth or the thread. Her stitching is worse than mine.

"I never could fool you, Ki-Yaga. What gave me away?"

Sensei points to the knots in the tassel on Lu Zeng's belt. Monkey fist knots! So that's what Lu Zeng meant about clever fingers.

"A work of art. Such precision." Lu Zeng holds the tassel up for us to admire. "It was a pleasant surprise to find my captive so talented."

"It's a knot," Mikko says with a snort.

"Not just any knot, young samurai. An extremely powerful one. The knots in a thread are years in a man's life. If the knots do not come undone, a man might live forever."

Mikko laughs until he sees the look on Sensei's face.

"It is true. How long is a life? How long is a piece of string?" our teacher asks. "It is the same question."

And Kyoko's knots never come undone. No wonder Lu Zeng wants his life string in her hands.

"Is that what you want now?" Sensei asks Lu Zeng. "To live forever? It can't be done."

"Maybe not. But at least I will outlive you," Lu Zeng gloats. "I am not hampered by foolish notions of honor. If another must bleed for me, so be it. My life is worth more than theirs."

Sensei shakes his head and pulls his beard. "The counting of years does not matter. Time is better spent counting grains of rice. At least in the end, you will make a good soup."

"Our emperor agrees with me. He has rewarded my studies with riches and power because I can help him live longer."

"It seems to me if the Son of Heaven wants to extend his life, he should ask his King above, not you," suggests Sensei.

Lu Zeng snarls. "Men have had their heads lopped off for saying less."

I am tired of all this talk. I came to rescue Kyoko, not to listen to old men argue.

"You are nothing but a coward," I accuse Lu Zeng. "Anyone who kidnaps and terrorizes children, threatens to cut them into pieces, does not deserve to live another day."

"You don't frighten us," Yoshi says. "You are not worthy to challenge our master."

No one plans better than Yoshi, and Lu Zeng rushes straight into the trap. His eyes blaze at the insult. A man whose eyes are on fire cannot see past the flames.

"One last test," Sensei says softly. "You choose. If I win, I take Kyoko, and you may keep my jade seal. If I lose, they are both yours."

But that's not fair, I think.

I will not need the seal again. Sensei's eyes gleam. *It is an offer Lu Zeng cannot resist.*

"Meet me at my palace. Tomorrow after breakfast. If you can get past the guard at my door." Lu Zeng laughs. "I will consult the tortoise oracle, and its dragon-bone pieces of shell will guide me in the choice of contest." Lu Zeng turns toward the central door. "You will lose, old man. You may even die."

His laughter hangs in the air and rankles in our hearts long after Lu Zeng has left.

Sensei raises his eyebrows. "I will not live forever, but I will certainly live longer than tomorrow. No matter what any tortoise says."

"How can we trust him?" asks Yoshi.

"We can't. We must return to the outer city to prepare. Lu Zeng might talk to tortoises for advice, but I need to speak with Master Jang," our teacher says.

Yoshi hesitates. "I don't like leaving Kyoko with Lu Zeng."

"He won't hurt her," Sensei says. "He needs her."

Our master's words give us comfort and untie the knots in my stomach. The square is deserted. We trace our steps back through the gates, along the central avenue, and up the stairs to Master Jang's house.

He greets us at the door. "I have been expecting you, my friends. Come in. Come in."

"I must speak with Master Jang in private," our master tells us.

"What will we do while you talk?" asks Taji.

Sensei grins.

We know what that means. "More practice," we chorus.

"You must each work on your weakness. Tomorrow Lu Zeng will seek it out," Sensei advises.

We head to the courtyard to practice while Sensei and Master Jang plot inside.

"Perhaps Sensei will poison Lu Zeng," says Mikko, hopefully.

It's an awful way to die, but Lu Zeng deserves it.

Yoshi shakes his head. "Sensei will not stoop to play by Lu Zeng's rules. He will find an honorable way."

"I'm going to practice my sword thrusts," says Taji.

"I'll help you," offers Mikko. Even Sensei cannot match Mikko's swordsmanship.

Yoshi takes the ninja dagger from his belt. "My throwing could do with improvement." He looks at me.

"I think I'll go for a walk," I say, heading for the door.

My weakness is not in my sword arm or throwing technique or even my one-legged stance. It's in the dark corner of my heart, where the White Crane fidgets, unable to find peace.

"Don't go too far," Yoshi calls. "Be careful."

Out on the street, I am all alone. Free to think. I find myself a cool, sheltered spot beside a fountain and close my eyes. The White Crane likes the wet rustle of running water. It sounds like home.

Sensei says that no one is ever truly alone. But I am.

Here on the streets of Beijing, there is no one to call me by name. No familiar face to look upon.

"Hello, friend samurai."

I open my eyes to find that Sensei is right. Of course.

"Hello, Chen," I say. "How is your arm?"

"Mending well. The scar is earning me great respect in the streets."

He sits down beside me, stretching out his feet.

"You've got new boots," I notice.

"Yes. I know a man who has too many to store away, so I helped him with his problem. I left my other boots at Master Jang's door. I appreciate what your teacher did for me, but I like to settle my own debts. It is a matter of honor."

"Sensei would understand that. He thinks honor is very important."

Honor is a strange thing, too. Everyone has their own way of looking at it.

"*Chi, jin, yu,*" I murmur.

"What's that?" Chen asks.

"Wisdom, benevolence, and courage. The code of the samurai."

"Be clever, be kind, be brave. I like that saying," says Chen. "Do you think one day your master might teach me such things?"

I shrug. "I don't know, but he said you were welcome at the Cockroach Ryu. It is the first step, and you cannot go anywhere without taking it."

We sit in silence.

"Why are you here all alone?" he finally asks.

"I came to sit and think where I would not be interrupted."

"Oh. Sorry," Chen says. "I'll be quiet."

But that's not easy for Chen.

"Sometimes it helps to talk. Perhaps you could tell me what bothers you," he says.

What have I got to lose?

"It's my friend Yoshi."

"The big kid?"

"Yes. He used to be like a brother to me, but recently, things have changed. He's keeping a secret."

Silence again. Chen waits, then realizes I've got nothing else to add.

"Is that it?" he says.

"It's very important to me."

"In the alleys of Beijing, we have a saying of our own. 'The things you care about must be let go. If they come back, it was meant to be.'"

"And if it doesn't come back?" I ask.

"It was never there in the first place."

I understand what he means. Sensei has been telling me the same thing ever since Yoshi returned from the White Tiger Temple. Yoshi is my friend, so I must trust him.

"Thanks, Chen. That's good advice."

But Chen hasn't finished yet.

"Does Yoshi know everything about you?"

I think a minute, then shake my head. "No. But this time it's different. Sensei knows the secret, so why is Yoshi excluding me?"

"Do you and your master share a secret?"

I nod. My friends don't know I can hear Sensei's voice inside my head. They wouldn't understand. They laugh when I suggest that Sensei knows things no ordinary man would. They tease me with the village stories about Sensei and the *tengu*. If I told them I heard voices, they would torment me even more.

"See? Everyone has secrets." Chen taps my forehead. "You have secrets you keep hidden from Yoshi."

I never thought of it like that before. His words eat into the darkness inside me, and the White Crane shakes its feathers in the new light. I feel free. As if I could fly away.

"I'm supposed to be practicing with the others," I say. "Do you want to join us?"

He nods happily.

"Look who I met in the street," I call into the courtyard.

My friends crowd around, pleased that Chen is well again.

"Show us your scar." Mikko is eager to look.

Chen lifts his jacket sleeve. Whistling in admiration, Taji runs his fingers down the ridge on Chen's arm.

"It is a mark worthy of a swordsman," says Yoshi.

Chen shakes his sleeve back into place. "Thank you. I was hoping I might learn a few samurai skills now that my arm is stronger."

"I don't know," Mikko jokes. "This is a Lin courtyard. You have to pay first. I think I need new shoes."

"Perhaps you could teach Mikko how to speak Chinese properly," suggests Taji. "That would be a fair payment."

"It wouldn't be fair at all. It will take years to teach Mikko," I say, teasing.

"Then I will show you all the Game of Five Elements," offers Chen.

We nod. Games are fun, and we could do with some of that.

"There are five elements—fire, water, metal, wood, and earth. One to match each finger." Chen holds up a digit as he names each element.

We nod again. Sensei would like this game, too. Five is his favorite number. And there are five of us.

"Fire burns wood. Water puts out fire. And so on. Each element has a strength and a weakness. I say, 'Five elements go,' and someone holds out a finger. Then we see whose finger is the strongest element. Who wants to play first?"

"I will," says Yoshi.

"Five elements go," calls Chen.

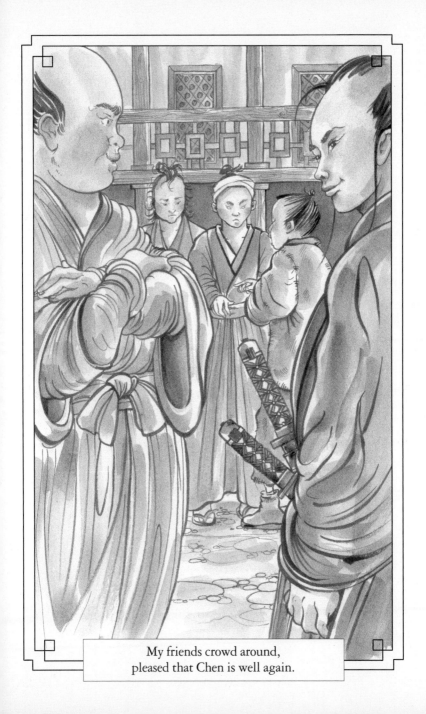

My friends crowd around,
pleased that Chen is well again.

Yoshi holds out his index finger, and Chen his thumb. Water beats fire. Yoshi wins.

"Go, Yoshi!" I yell, punching the air with my fist. I stumble backward and into Sensei, who has just walked in with our evening meal.

"Master Jang has prepared supper," our teacher says. Six red bowls rest on the tray. One for Chen, too. Somehow Sensei knew there was an extra mouth to feed.

"Is it okay if I sit here?" I ask Yoshi, pointing to the space beside him.

"You never have to ask." He smiles.

I see you have worked on your weakness as I instructed. Excellent, Niya. Sensei smiles, picking a bamboo shoot from his teeth. *Now we are ready to face Lu Zeng.*

It is still hard to trust, but Chen has helped me, I admit.

I know. The boy is destined for greater things than this city can offer.

Looking up, Chen sees us watching and grins.

By morning, Chen has disappeared back into the busy streets. We wander among carts piled high with food. Pancakes filled with egg and vegetables. Sweet dumplings. Twists of deep-fried dough. My stomach hesitates, but this morning my heart is in charge. I want to go straight to Lu Zeng's palace.

"I can't eat knowing that Kyoko is Lu Zeng's prisoner. I can't wait a moment longer. Let's go now," I say.

"I'm not hungry, either," says Taji.

But Sensei insists we fill our stomachs first. "An empty stomach is as useless as an empty head."

The noodle pancakes are soft and warm, but they stick in my throat as if they are days old. My friends are in a hurry, too, and eat as quickly as possible. But in the end, it makes no difference. We have to wait for Sensei to finish, and even though he is as skinny as a flagpole, he eats twice as much as Yoshi.

Finally, he sucks his fingers clean, wiping them on his beard. "I am ready."

We make our way through the now-familiar system of gates. Crossing the right bridge. Choosing the correct tunnel.

"It is rare for the Emperor to give a palace to a government official," says Sensei. "We must be very careful where we walk. We do not want to tread on imperial toes."

Lu Zeng's palace is small but grander than anywhere we've ever been before. The entrance pathway is paved with carved marble, and the door is flanked by bronze tortoises and two enormous vats of water in case of fire. Every year lightning strikes at least one of the wooden buildings of the Forbidden City. Even the Hall of Supreme Harmony has been set alight.

In the distance, we see that the great red door is protected by nine rows of nine gold bolts. Nine is a lucky number in China. A guard is blocking our way to the door. Round and well fed, he seems more interested in the game of dice he is playing than in doing his job. He probably hasn't raised his weapon for years. Maybe we *are* in luck.

"What should we do?" Mikko asks.

"We must use our heads," Sensei instructs. "Let your head lead your sword."

Mikko grins. "Then I know what to do."

Before I have a chance to ask, Mikko slides toward the guard. The only sound a lizard makes is a rustle in the grass. On the grassless palace steps, the Striped Gecko is completely silent.

Crack.

Mikko brings the flat blade of his sword down hard on the guard's head. The man crumples like a bag of bean seed.

"No harm done," Mikko calls softly. "I used his head to lead my sword."

It's a good solution all around. The guard is disabled, and we can walk through. He'll have a lump on his head in the morning, but he is lucky because, unlike Master Jang's victims, he'll live to eat another breakfast.

When we reach the door, it is not even closed. We are expected.

"I didn't have to hit the guard over the head after all." Mikko looks guilty. Perhaps because we know he enjoyed it.

"Your effort was not wasted," says Sensei. "You have taught the guard to be more watchful in the future. If Lu Zeng caught him not paying attention, his punishment would not be as gentle as a knock on the head. You probably saved the man's life."

Mikko beams as he swaggers through the door into a small courtyard.

We stop suddenly, entranced.

It's as if Lu Zeng has moved a mountain. Miniature

waterfalls and trees, natural rock sculptures green with moss, the whirr of cicadas. In the pond, red and white carp swim between lotus blossoms.

"It's so peaceful." I dip my finger in the water. "How could a man as wicked as Lu Zeng have created something as lovely as this?"

"It is the way," Sensei says. "The way of the Tao. Yin and yang. Dark and light cannot exist without each other. No one is truly bad or truly good. We all have a little darkness inside." He looks directly at me. "We all make mistakes."

I know, and now my darkness is fading.

"Lu Zeng made a big mistake when he stole Kyoko," Mikko says. "It won't be a peaceful meeting when he faces us."

The room empties into a short corridor. At the next door, six soldiers with tortoise emblems on their chests greet us. Lu Zeng's personal guard. They stand to attention when they see us and bow to Sensei.

At least we don't have to fight our way in here.

"Jin Shi," they greet in unison.

"Welcome, learned one. You are expected," the first guard says.

"Twice welcome," adds another. "Your visit has put our noble lord in a good mood, and we are grateful for that. Look"—he waves toward a nearby table—"even a morning meal has been provided for us today."

Lu Zeng is celebrating his victory in advance. It's a bad move. Overconfidence is a great handicap, Sensei teaches. It is easy to outwit a man who is not paying attention because he thinks he has already won.

"I would be honored to contribute to your feast." Sensei takes a bottle from underneath his jacket. We've seen it before, at Master Jang's house.

"This is a rare Japanese wine. It's a little bitter at first, but if you are the equal of a samurai, I am sure you will find the stomach for it."

"One Middle Kingdom soldier is the equal of five samurai," the first declares. "We will fill our cups to the brim and drink deep."

Surely, Sensei is not going to poison these men. They are only doing their duty, and I bet it's not often a pleasant one with a master like Lu Zeng.

"In you go," a guard says, waving us through. "One should not keep Lu Zeng waiting, even when he is in a good mood."

"What was in the bottle?" I ask Taji. "I couldn't smell anything."

"Don't worry, Niya. It was only a sleeping potion," he says.

That's a relief, but I'm still nervous. I'm sure the beauty of the first room is only an illusion to fool the casual visitor. I'll bet that whatever is beyond this door is sure to be ugly.

And I'm right.

As the door swings open, a low growl escapes from Yoshi's lips.

"What's wrong?" I ask.

He dips his head, and my eyes follow. Many spirits are imprisoned in Lu Zeng's lair. A white tiger skin, beaten, flattened, and tacked to the wall. Tortoise shells, cracked and broken into pieces. Snake and lizard skins. Stuffed carcasses. A crane stands beside a grotesquely bent bat. Butterflies in the hundreds hang from pins.

All our spirit animals are there—all except Kyoko's. And where is Kyoko herself? Is there somewhere else, even worse than this?

CHAPTER TEN

名誉

MONKEY MOVES

"I have come for my student!" Sensei's voice booms through the palace.

"Then come. You are welcome in my Room of Science." Lu Zeng's words come from the shadows, but they are mellow and warm. Inviting.

How can a man so cold and evil have such a voice? And why doesn't he come out so we can see him?

"Leave your swords at the door," the voice instructs.

"We cannot do that," Sensei politely refuses.

He does not trust this man. None of us do.

"Then I will have my guards remove them for you," threatens Lu Zeng.

Sensei laughs. "You do not have enough guards to take even one samurai's sword, and we are five. Perhaps you remember it is my favorite number."

When we played the game of five elements with Chen, metal didn't always win.

But I know it will here.

"I give my word. I will not raise my sword unless yours is raised first," Sensei promises. "Now, where is my student? It is time for you to show yourself and honor your word."

But Lu Zeng is not a man of honor. Again the bodiless

laughter echoes through the room. "Find me and you will find her. But I warn you, I am a master of conceal-ment, and even Lin tricks will not help you now. I can easily hide from you."

"Where is my student?" Sensei demands again. His voice strikes the walls like a gong, echoing loud. This time there is no answer.

Eyebrows raised, Sensei smiles and presses his fingers together to form a temple. "It seems we must play one last game of hide-and-seek. I do not understand why Lu Zeng is so eager to lose again."

A long passageway leads from the Room of Science. There are many closed doors on both sides.

"Taji, Mikko, and I will search the eastern half of the palace. Niya and Yoshi will go west," decides Sensei.

"Don't worry, Sensei," Yoshi says. "We'll find Kyoko and Enlai."

"And Lu Zeng," Mikko adds.

Sensei grins. "We are not looking for any of *them.*"

"Then what *are* we looking for?" asks Taji.

"Tortoises," Sensei announces with a flourish of his traveling staff.

Now we are all confused.

"Lu Zeng is a moving target. It is a waste of my breath to chase him all over this palace where the walls and corridors will be pocked with secret doors and compartments. We will wait for him to come to us. Eventually, he must feed his beloved tortoises. And when he does, he will discover us there. We need to find which door hides the Tortoise Room."

It's a clever plan but even though I'm interested to see what the rooms of a palace look like, I am desperate to see Kyoko.

The first door Yoshi and I look in is a small storage cupboard. Nothing but bags of wheat and rice packed against jars of honey, jam, and dried peaches.

"Sensei might be looking for tortoises," confides Yoshi, "but I'm looking for Kyoko."

"Me too."

Yoshi and I always think the same, even if things aren't quite back to normal between us.

The next door opens to reveal a bedroom. Everything is black. Even the curtain of knots draped in a canopy across the bed. Perhaps Lu Zeng thinks it will help him grow younger as he sleeps.

"I'll look under the bed," Yoshi says. "You look in the cupboards."

We search with our swords drawn. All the rooms are empty. Even the kitchen is eerily silent. The floor is scuffed with busy footprints, but there are no servants here today.

At the sixth door, we both stop. The room smells of blood.

"I don't want to go in," I whisper.

"Me either," says Yoshi.

I know we're both thinking the same thing again. What if Kyoko is behind this door? What if it's her blood we can smell, and we open the door to discover her body?

"We could get Sensei first," I suggest.

Yoshi shakes his head. "We might not have time."

He's right. While we talk, Kyoko might be bleeding to death.

I place my hand on the door handle. Yoshi places his hand over mine. Together, we are brave. With a great heave, we fling the door open.

Kyoko is nowhere to be seen. And neither is Enlai.

Our relief is soon stifled by the thick, sweet smell of death. A pile of small animal carcasses, mostly bats and mice, covers the table in the center of the room. Some have no heads. Some have been slit from neck to tail, their body cavities empty.

Maps and diagrams cover the walls. Drawings of skeletons and bones, muscles and organs. A grotesque gallery of animals, birds, and people. Things a man could only know by looking beneath the skin.

"I think we should get Sensei after all," says Yoshi. "Are you okay to stay here?"

I nod. I am not afraid. I am angry. The White Crane beats its wings against my chest. I want to tear the room into such small pieces that no one could ever put them back together again.

"This is Lu Zeng's Room of Experiments." Our master sadly shakes his head as he enters. "But it is no place of science. This is a place of great suffering."

"It's evil here," says Taji, looking toward the heap of dismembered bats. He can't see them, but he knows they are there.

Sensei carefully removes some of the diagrams from the wall. "I am sure Master Jang would be able to put these to better use. He will use them to save lives. There is nothing else I want to see again. Let us close these doors and continue our search."

"I'd like to make sure these doors are closed forever," I mutter.

"Someone should burn this palace down." Mikko's eyes flash, and if the flames there could escape, the fire would be already lit.

Yoshi slams the door shut behind us.

The corridor is lined with potted bamboo. My mother says that if you put bamboo in your home, you will have a long and happy life. Maybe that's why Lu Zeng has the plants here, but I shudder to think what would make a man like that happy. Mikko and I poke each bamboo clump with our swords to make sure he is not hiding behind them.

Our search progresses slowly. What was interesting and exciting to begin with is now repetitive and boring.

Until Mikko shouts, "Tortoises. I've found tortoises."

There are tortoises everywhere in the room. Even the table base is a great bronze tortoise. There are tanks and fountains, paintings and pottery. In this room at least, life is treated with respect. Sensei was right. It is the perfect place to sit and wait.

We don't have to wait long.

The calm is soon broken by Lu Zeng, his black cloak billowing behind him like a storm cloud. His face is filled with thunder, and his voice crashes through the air. "Why are you sitting here? Why aren't you looking for me?"

"But I am," Sensei says. "And now I have found you." He rises from the tortoise-shell chair to stare Lu Zeng in the face. "I will ask one more time. Where is my student?"

"She was under your nose from the beginning," Lu Zeng gloats. "You are not as good at finding things as you think. Come and I will show you how shortsighted you have become."

He couldn't be more wrong. Sensei knows what will happen before it comes to pass. He can see great distances, all the way into the future.

We follow Lu Zeng back to the first room. Tugging on a knotted silk rope pulley, he rolls back a section of the roof, and a cage descends from above the ceiling. Kyoko is sitting behind the bars. Like a bird. Her mouth is taped shut.

How dare he? If only Sensei would let me draw my sword.

Lu Zeng rips the tape from Kyoko's mouth, and it's even harder to hold back my anger.

But Kyoko has her own complaints to make.

"Where have you been?" she demands of us. "I've been waiting for ages."

I'm so glad to see her. Even her complaints ring in my ears like birdsong.

Sensei claps his hands together before Kyoko can continue berating us. "So, Lu Zeng, what did your dragon bones tell you?"

Lu Zeng smirks. "That I should return your student if you could answer one question."

That won't be hard. Sensei knows everything. More than any reading of tortoiseshell pieces.

"Ask me."

Lu Zeng's eyes glitter like a wet spiderweb. Danger lurks in his question. "Where have the monks from the White Tiger Temple gone?"

Sensei shakes his head.

But Lu Zeng persists. "I know you were there. I know they have sent the most skilled monks into hiding. This

Kyoko is sitting behind the bars. Like a bird.
Her mouth is taped shut.

is the question the dragon bones decreed. And an answer the Emperor will pay well to hear."

I *hate* dragons. Even their tortoiseshell bones cause us trouble.

"Tell me where the monks are," Lu Zeng insists, "or I'll kill the girl. I don't need her anymore, now that I can create my own knots." He holds up a length of string, expertly twisted and tied.

Lu Zeng waves the knots in Sensei's face. "Where are the White Tiger monks?"

Tell him, I scream.

But Sensei says nothing.

Tell him, I beg. *Mei, Du Feng, and the others will find a new place before the soldiers get there. They'll manage to escape, but Kyoko has no chance of getting away.*

Sensei shakes his head. *We cannot sacrifice one for many. No matter how bright Kyoko shines in our hearts.*

I bite my lip. Why doesn't Yoshi speak? His face is frozen, unyielding. I look at him pleadingly, but nothing melts. He would never disobey Sensei.

Taji and Mikko wait. Trusting our teacher.

Lu Zeng whirls to catch the panicked expression on my face.

"Ah. You will tell me!" He grins, triumphant. "There is always one who cares too deeply. It is a weakness to let your heart rule your head. To save her life, you will tell me what I want to know."

I would, if only I could. If there was any chance at all that Kyoko would be spared. But I don't know the answer.

"They wouldn't tell me," I mutter.

Slamming his fist against the table, Lu Zeng shouts at Sensei. "Stubborn fool! I won't kill her. That would be much too easy. I want to see you suffer."

Sensei is not worried. He smiles. *See, now no one is dead.*

No thanks to me. My words would have killed Mei and Du Feng as sure as any sword stroke. Now I understand why Sensei wouldn't let Yoshi tell me the secret. Sensei knew I would always choose Kyoko. A little knowledge can be a dangerous thing. As deadly as Master Jang's favorite poison.

"Sorry," I mouth to Yoshi. "I'm so stupid sometimes."

He grins. I guess he knew that. "Blood brothers always," he mouths in return.

Lu Zeng is not grinning. "Let us solve our differences

the traditional way. One of your champions against one of mine. A fight with sticks until only one is left standing. Is that acceptable to you?"

Sensei shrugs. "My student will win."

Lu Zeng grins now. "Then it does not matter if I choose the champions for both of us."

"I am not bothered by that." Sensei shrugs again.

"You," he points at me, "will fight for Ki-Yaga."

I bow my head. "I am honored."

He probably thinks one leg will make me easy to beat. I'm not our best *bo* fighter, but I'm good enough to defeat any soldier. Let Lu Zeng call the captain of the Emperor's Imperial Guard. I'm ready.

"For my champion, I choose . . ." Lu Zeng's eyes sweep around the room to rest on Kyoko. "Her."

I'm not ready for that. Honor turns to ash in my mouth.

"But she is not yours to choose," I sputter. I look to Sensei for help, but he shakes his head.

"My student will win," he repeats.

Sensei is right of course. But I don't understand. The expressions on the faces of my friends tell me they are confused, too.

Lu Zeng laughs so hard he clutches at his stomach. "Yes, one of your students will win, but either way, you lose, Ki-Yaga. If the girl wins, she stays here. If the boy wins, you will suffer with every strike he makes."

He opens the cage, and Kyoko climbs down.

I can't hear her voice in my head, but I can read the message in her eyes. *Don't worry, Niya,* she is saying, *I trust you.*

It's more than I did for Yoshi.

Lu Zeng takes a tall wooden pole from the corner and passes it to Kyoko. Sensei places his traveling staff in my hands.

I'm not even sure I *can* beat Kyoko. We practice together all the time, and she wins as often as I do.

Halfheartedly, I swing the staff. Kyoko fends it away. We circle around, feinting and dodging.

"If you do not fight," Lu Zeng reminds me, "I will win."

I kick toward Kyoko, who catches at my foot. And misses. Any other time, she would have tripped me over.

Hunching both shoulders, she slouches into monkey

posture. I know all the monkey moves the Shaolin monks taught her, but that doesn't make it easier. Muscles tensed, heart shaking, I hold Sensei's staff ready for the quick upward stroke. *Thwack.* Our poles vibrate with the power of the clash. But our fight is just a well-choreographed dance. How long can we keep pretending?

What can I do? I ask Sensei.

If you must beat Kyoko, it would be best if she didn't feel it, he says.

How?

She should go to sleep.

That's no help at all.

Kyoko lets her arm hang loose. I know this one well. The monkey fist punch. It would be enough to knock me out if it connected. But I can't be the one to sleep. If only I could use my finger. Like Sensei does. You have to really want to, he said. I've never wanted anything more in my whole life.

Wedging her staff into the ground, Kyoko uses it as a base to vault toward me, smiling as if all I have to do is catch her. If only that were true.

And suddenly I realize it is. As she strikes against me,

I take all of our weight against my staff, pressing my fingers hard into her neck. She drops like a sack of rice at my feet. Out cold.

"My student wins," announces Sensei. *I told you so,* his smile taunts Lu Zeng. "Here is the jade seal I promised. Now I will take Kyoko away with me. Do not try to stop us."

"Guards!" Lu Zeng shouts.

"You do not have enough guards to stand in our way. And today you have none. Your guards are sleeping. It seems I have learned something from your tactics, and the tricks of the Lin are useful to me after all."

Yoshi gathers Kyoko into his arms. Glaring, daring Lu Zeng to try and stop him. "Our teacher would never let anyone hurt one of his students," he says.

Lu Zeng laughs. Sensei says laughter heals the soul, but there is something twisted and corrupt about Lu Zeng's laugh. It hurts down inside my eardrums.

"They don't know, do they?" he sneers at Sensei. And then he laughs again. "You haven't told them what you did. Have you?"

"No," Sensei says. And for the first time, he looks defeated.

"Whatever it was, we don't care," Yoshi says.

I wouldn't believe Lu Zeng anyway. "Don't waste your time telling us," I snap.

We all stand together to defend our teacher.

"We know our own master well enough," insists Taji.

Mikko glares. "And we are not interested in what you know."

"Oh, I'm not going to say anything." Lu Zeng smirks. "The more time that passes, the deeper it will cut when you learn your master's terrible secret." He claps his hands together in glee. "I shall have my revenge yet. I don't even need this."

He throws the jade seal at our master's feet, and Mikko hurries to pick it up. We leave the palace, finally together.

Out in the street, Sensei stops, turning to face us. "It is true that I have a dark secret. If you ask me, I will tell you. I will not hide it from you any longer."

I've waited a long time for this moment. I've hoped Sensei would tell me his dark secret. Hoped I would be able to help him.

But I know now, this is not the way it should be. I

have learned my lesson. Yoshi's hand on my shoulder gives me new strength.

"No," I say. "When the time is right, you will tell us and we will not need to ask."

Sometimes a secret is like a little stick. At first it annoys you and pokes in your sandal. Then it grows and the edge sharpens until it feels like a dagger, but now I know there is another way. You can take the stick out of your shoe and carry it in your pocket like a small sprig of cherry branch to blossom when it is ready.

I shake my head and tuck the imaginary sprig in my pocket along with the peach stone Master Jang gave me.

"The past is long gone," Taji says. "Whatever happened doesn't matter."

Sensei shakes his head. "It does matter. It matters a great deal."

"It doesn't matter to us," I insist. "And when the time comes, you will do what needs to be done, and we will be there to help you."

"The past is just a path to the future, and no man can choose his path," Mikko says.

We all look at him with surprise. Who would have thought Mikko would remember a lesson? I didn't even think he paid that much attention.

But Sensei looks most surprised. "You are right. A teacher can always learn from his students."

"Especially a student as good as me," Mikko says with a grin.

In Yoshi's arms, Kyoko stirs. I reach out and gently touch the bruise on her neck.

"She'll be all right," says Taji.

Yes. Even a kid who is blind can see that.

CHAPTER ELEVEN

忠
誠

SPIDER BITE

It's a long wait for Kyoko to open her eyes. The sun goes to bed and gets up again. Still Kyoko sleeps.

"When is she going to wake up?" Yoshi asks.

What if she never does? No one asks that.

But I'm worried now. "I didn't hurt her, did I?"

"No. We must be patient," Sensei counsels. "Kyoko waited many days for us to come. Now we must wait for her. She has much more to recover from than her fight with Niya. She has been in a very dark place."

"We'll have to watch out for Niya's fingers in the future," Mikko says, trying to cheer me up. "No more pinching."

"I don't think I could do it again," I murmur.

"You can because you are different now. There is powerful *ki* in your fingertips," says Sensei.

Carefully, I inspect my hands. They look the same to me. "What does that mean?"

Sensei smiles. "It means you should be careful where you point."

We take turns watching Kyoko. While the others practice in the courtyard, Sensei and I sit at her bedside.

I am glad you are here with me, I say to my teacher. Somehow it means more without the words.

It is good, he replies.

"Are there many others who can share thoughts like we do?" I ask, remembering Qing-Shen speaking inside my head. The White Crane shivers and fluffs its feathers. It didn't like listening to Qing-Shen at all.

"I have known only three," says Sensei.

"If one was Qing-Shen, who was the other?"

"The first student I ever taught. It was a long time ago." Sensei shakes his head. "I was young then and not ready to teach. I was not as wise as you are now."

"Perhaps one day I will be even wiser than you." I grin. "Especially if I have a head start."

"I hope you are, Little Cockroach." Sensei pats me on the shoulder. "Then I shall retire to sleep in the sun."

What is so different about that?

We laugh together. Sometimes I feel as if Sensei and I are connected. But it's a very fine line, and whenever I look hard to find it, it's not there at all.

"What happened to your first student?" I ask, settling back. Our teacher says that all his students are destined for greatness. This should be a good tale.

But Sensei's smile fades. "There is nothing to tell."

There is. I can see the story in the sadness of his eyes.

It's one more secret for Sensei to keep, but that's okay. I understand about secrets now.

"We are only human. We all make mistakes," I remind him.

"Yes," he sighs. "They haunt us like nightmares when we try to sleep. And sometimes they make us even less human."

He looks tired. As if he needs a good sleep.

I want to tell him that I'll always be there for him. But you can't promise what you don't know. Sensei wouldn't value an empty promise, anyway. I reach out and touch his arm to show my support.

It isn't enough. I throw my arms around him, hugging tightly.

"If you keep that up, my bones will be crushed to powder. Perhaps then Master Jang will use it in a potion," my teacher says.

But he hugs me back, just as hard.

Kyoko opens one eye then the other. Then she winks.

"Kyoko is awake!" I cheer. And she's as mischievous as ever.

Our friends come running.

"What took you so long? I was stuck in that cage for days," Kyoko complains.

It's as close to a thank-you as we're going to get.

She flexes her fingers, cracking all six knuckles on each hand. "My hands almost dropped off tying those knots while I waited for you boys to rescue me."

I breathe a great sigh of relief. Nothing has changed. Not even Lu Zeng could destroy Kyoko's spirit.

"I don't know why we had to rescue you at all. Surely, a girl samurai doesn't need our help to escape from a few kidnappers?" Yoshi teases. "How many were there? Ten?"

Kyoko wrinkles her nose. "Three," she admits.

"Only three," Taji whoops. "I could have escaped with my eyes closed."

"A *boy* would have seen a way to escape," boasts Mikko.

But he doesn't see Kyoko move. Quick as a snake, her arm flashes out to wrap around Mikko's neck.

"Help!" he sputters.

"What, you can escape three kidnappers but not one girl?" challenges Kyoko.

"Make her let go," Mikko begs.

But we're not stupid. We're not going anywhere within Kyoko's reach. Even Sensei shrugs.

"Say it: Kyoko is smarter than any samurai boy."

Mikko squirms in her grasp.

"Say it!" she insists.

"All right." Mikko relents. "Kyoko is smarter than any samurai boy."

"Yell it."

She squeezes, and Mikko yells as loud as he can.

Poor Mikko. He never learns not to annoy Kyoko.

"That's better." She releases him. "I missed you, Mikko. You are such fun."

"I'm glad you're back, too," he says, rubbing his neck.

"We were all very worried about you. Were you frightened?" Yoshi asks Kyoko.

She shakes her head. "I knew you would come, but it was a horrible place to wait. I tried to close my eyes and cover my ears, but it was never enough."

"Lu Zeng's Room of Experiments made me cold all over. I'm glad I couldn't see it," says Taji.

"Sometimes I felt so empty that I cried," Kyoko whispers. "Then I would think about our mountains and imagine I was there."

"I felt sick not knowing where you were," I mutter.

"It's true," says Mikko. "He didn't even eat his first helping of honey rice pudding."

Kyoko smiles, but suddenly her expression changes.

"We have to go back. Right now." She drags herself up. The memories are pouring back, faster than the Yellow River when it is flooded. "There was a boy imprisoned with me. He's only seven, but he's brave enough to be a samurai kid." Her voice drops to a frightened whisper. "Lu Zeng is going to kill him. He wants to dissect his body." Kyoko starts to cry.

"We know," Sensei says, placing his arm around her and pulling her down next to him. "His name is Enlai. I have promised his grandfather I will rescue him. I won't let anything happen to him."

The sobs stop, but Kyoko is still shaking. "The boy said his people were leaving the city. He was afraid they would go without him."

"How do you know all this?" Yoshi asks. "We were told Enlai can't speak."

She smiles weakly and holds up her hand. "Six fingers are useful for more than tying knots. We made hand signals, and Enlai knows well enough how to get his message across. He bit Lu Zeng."

He really is brave. Or desperate. Or frightened. Maybe all three.

"We need to go now," Kyoko implores. "He'll die if we don't free him."

Sensei tugs at his beard, the way he does when he is thinking hard. "We cannot rush back to rescue Enlai. Lu Zeng will be expecting us, and we do not want to get caught in his trap."

That's for sure. We saw the butterflies and moths impaled on pins. And the beetles and earwigs stuck to paper scrolls. We definitely don't want Lu Zeng to add Little Cockroaches to his collection.

"We will go tonight, when our Chinese Lin and Owl Ninja skills will be at their best advantage. Now that we have taken Kyoko back, Lu Zeng will have hidden Enlai well away. He will not risk losing a third game of hide-and-seek," Sensei says. "But first Kyoko must rest."

She tries to rise again, but Sensei gently pulls her back. "If you do not rest, you will not be able to come with us tonight. I have a potion from Master Jang to help you recover."

"Yuck." Kyoko doesn't like the smell or the taste, but she swallows it anyway and falls fast asleep until lunchtime. And as soon as she wakes, she is up to her old tricks.

"Can't we go outside, Master?" she asks.

Yoshi is nervous and unsure. "Lu Zeng swore to assassinate Sensei if we rescued you."

"I am not afraid of Lu Zeng." Kyoko makes a monkey fist with her hand.

"We are not afraid," says Taji. "Just careful."

"Can we at least explore the city a bit?" Kyoko asks. "We will soon leave Beijing, and I won't have seen a single street stall. Please," she says, twisting Sensei around her finger like a piece of string. Tying us all in knots.

I want to make Kyoko happy, but I don't want to do anything to endanger Sensei.

"Can Lu Zeng hurt you, Master?" I ask.

"Of course not. It is not my time to die. Besides, I have not finished teaching yet." He smiles. "Sometimes I think my students know NOTHING."

It's a huge compliment.

"Does that mean we can go?" asks Kyoko. "One day I managed to look out the window and watch the people flying kites from their rooftops. I only glimpsed snatches of color but it was the brightest thing I saw while I was imprisoned. Now I want to fly a kite to celebrate the wind and being free."

"I'd like to see the kites," Yoshi says.

"Me too," adds Mikko.

"Another day, I heard a wonderful sound. It was like a bird call. More beautiful than any *shakuhachi* note I can play." Kyoko closes her eyes, listening. "Lu Zeng said the princesses tie whistles to the tails of pigeons then toss them up to hear the sound as they fly. He said it is a popular sport on the streets of Beijing, but I would never escape to see it."

"I'd like to hear the whistles," adds Taji.

"And I'd like to prove Lu Zeng wrong," I say.

Five pleading faces turn toward Sensei.

"We will spend two hours in the streets," he decides. "Then we must rest before rescuing Enlai."

In the marketplace, we meet up with Master Jang.

Sensei introduces Kyoko. "This is my student who has now returned to us."

"I am glad to see that you are better," says Master Jang, staring at her.

"What's wrong?" Kyoko asks.

"You have unusual hair. A knot made from its strands would be a talisman of great power. You are lucky Lu Zeng did not think of that."

Kyoko bows deep with respect. "I am twice lucky. I am also grateful for the medicine you provided."

Opening his pack, Sensei hands Master Jang the charts from the Room of Experiments. "I found these in Lu Zeng's palace. Please accept them as a gift in return for the *wodao*."

Master Jang grins. He understands and approves. Sensei doesn't owe him anything now.

"Thank you. You have a Lin soul. Please be careful where you go," he says. "Lu Zeng is like the spider. He sits and waits for what his web will bring him."

One moment Master Jang is waving good-bye, and the next, he disappears.

Along the street, vendors shout to the passersby. And everyone wants to sell something to a white-haired samurai girl.

"Someone is following us," Taji hisses.

"Perhaps it's Chen," I whisper hopefully.

Taji shakes his head. "It is not Chen. He might be

small, but he sneaks like an old water buffalo."

It's true. If Sensei decides to teach Chen, he has a lot of work ahead.

Taji tips his ear into the breeze. "The one who follows us is much larger, but he sneaks like a ninja."

We know what to do to sneak up on whoever is following us. The ninja at the Owl Dojo taught us how to creep with the wind and how to turn and catch the air blowing in our faces. Sensei leads us around and back to run right into our tail—Big Wu.

"Elder Lin asked me to protect you. He does not want you killed before you have had a chance to rescue his grandson," says Big Wu, his face red with embarrassment.

"You are a welcome bodyguard," says Sensei.

"You are welcome anytime," I say to our friend.

"Um," Big Wu says, looking even more uncomfortable, "perhaps you won't mention to Elder Lin that you discovered me following you?"

"We did?" Taji looks surprised. "The way I saw it, you came up to us."

Taji is always one step ahead. You don't need eyes to see the best path to follow.

"Come for a walk with us," Mikko offers. "We're going to see the kites."

Big Wu shakes his head. "But I will not be far behind you."

Taking a few steps back, he fades into the crowd. When the White Crane looks again, he is gone. Another Lin shadow.

"I would like to see inside the Emperor's palace," muses Kyoko. "Just a peek. Imagine how beautiful it must be."

Chinese people believe the God of Heaven lives on the Pole Star in a palace with ten thousand rooms. On Earth, the respectful son lives in the Forbidden City, with one less room than his father and a sleeping chamber of red and gold.

At home at the Cockroach Ryu, we all sleep together in one bedroom. You can't get more respectful than that.

"After we rescue Enlai, I would be happy if I never saw a palace ever again," I say. "I will never forget the horror of Lu Zeng's Room of Experiments."

"Riches, wealth, and power are dangerous weapons," Sensei agrees.

"Can I interest you in some sticky honey cakes?" asks a young baker, interrupting our conversation.

Even though we don't have any money, we look and sniff deeply. We're interested all right. The cakes smell sweet and promise to taste even better. Perhaps he might give us a sample.

"I think we should taste before we buy," says Kyoko, in a voice even sweeter than honey.

No one could resist her request. Leaning forward, the baker offers her a cake.

"Watch out!" someone yells.

The tray crashes. Cakes scatter.

The baker slumps across Taji, an arrow protruding from his back. Mikko helps Yoshi hurriedly lift the baker aside. But there's nothing we can do to help. Horrified, we watch as his face twitches into death's last lines.

We scramble to our feet. Scanning the crowd, I can't see anything suspicious.

"That's one of Master Jang's arrows," Sensei says, recognizing the shaft from our lesson a few days ago.

"Why would he want this man dead?" asks Kyoko.

We don't know. Even Sensei shrugs.

Big Wu strides up to us. "Elder Lin will be pleased with my work this afternoon."

He strips the man's sleeve back to reveal the poison

dart thrower laced to his arm. A Plum Flower Sleeve Arrow. Master Jang showed us one of those, too. The baker is an assassin and the darts were meant to kill us. Big Wu has saved our lives.

"There are four darts still in there," Mikko counts.

"That means two have been fired," says Taji.

"I hope the poison is not strong, because one dart has grazed my finger." Yoshi holds up his index finger. The thin scratch is already an ugly welt.

Sensei's face is grayer than the leftover ash in a fire.

"Taji, go and find Master Jang. Quickly. Tell him what happened. Mikko, bring the Sleeve Arrow. Master Jang will need to see the darts," Sensei says.

Big Wu has already scooped up Yoshi in his arms.

"I'm okay." Yoshi grins. But I can see the beads of perspiration on his forehead as he clamps his teeth tight to stop them from chattering. Lu Zeng has struck, after all. The Spider has bitten Yoshi.

Please don't let him die, I scream inside my head.

Be calm, Sensei answers. *Yoshi needs you.*

"What can I do?" I ask.

"Talk to Yoshi. You too, Kyoko." Sensei says. "Make sure Yoshi wants to live."

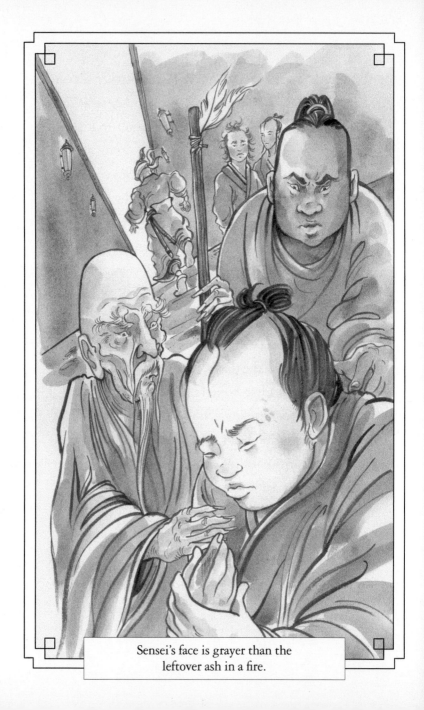

Sensei's face is grayer than the
leftover ash in a fire.

We rush to catch up to Big Wu.

"You are the Tiger," I whisper into my brother's ear. "There is no spirit as strong or brave. Your roar is loud enough to wake the dead. You know that, don't you?"

Yoshi doesn't answer. The Tiger is beyond roaring.

Carefully, Big Wu places Yoshi on the workbench. His injured hand is clenched tight. He moans as Master Jang straightens it to examine the finger. Mikko and I hold Yoshi's arm flat against the bench while Master Jang ties a tourniquet and places two needles in Yoshi's hand above the wound.

"This will help with the pain," Master Jang says. "Some of the poison has entered his blood."

Yoshi's eyes glaze over.

"It is best that he doesn't feel anything," Master Jang explains. "The dart was smeared with aconite. It is a very cruel poison." He looks at Sensei. "What do you offer as payment for the treatment?"

Lin honor. There is always a price to be paid. Even now.

"My jade seal," says Sensei.

It's worth a fortune.

But Master Jang shakes his head.

"My sword," I say without hesitation. It is my heart and soul, but I would gladly give it away for Yoshi's life.

Again, he shakes his head.

What does he want, then? What else do we have of value? We're wasting time.

"My hair. All of it," whispers Kyoko, pulling the pin from her topknot. "I will twist it into powerful knots for you."

Master Jang smiles. The trade is agreed.

He shakes Yoshi gently. Yoshi's eyes flicker open.

"You must trust me. Do you?" Master Jang whispers.

Yoshi looks to Sensei, who nods.

"I need to hear you say it." The Poisoner raises Yoshi's face toward his. "If you say it, I will end your pain."

Something about Master Jang's eyes makes me nervous. They are hard and dark. Concentrating, as if nothing exists except Yoshi's next word.

"Yes," he murmurs, slumping back onto the bench. Then he passes out.

Deep inside him, the Tiger is dying.

Master Jang's dagger glitters as it slices toward Yoshi.

CHAPTER TWELVE

義

WAY OF
THE WARRIOR

Kyoko gasps and clutches my arm for support. Wide-eyed, Mikko is frozen in place. Yoshi's severed finger lies on the bench beside his hand.

"Is he all right?" Taji asks.

"Master Jang c-cut Yoshi's finger off," I stammer.

"It had to be done," Sensei says. "It was the only way to stop the poison from spreading further. Thanks to Master Jang's quick work, Yoshi is still alive."

Yoshi moans, and his eyelids flutter. His breathing is loud but shallow. Every breath is a struggle. I feel powerless. All I can do is cross my fingers for him.

Deftly, Master Jang binds the stump with bandages soaked in red liquid.

"What's that?" Kyoko points to the soaking bowl.

"Dragon's blood," says Master Jang.

"Really?" Mikko leans over, interested.

"It will help stop the bleeding," says Sensei. "The Dragon is on our side now."

"It must be," says Master Jang. "Dragon's blood is made from the fruit of a rare palm tree, and I don't usually have any. Only yesterday I received a package from the South."

When we were studying at the Shaolin Temple,

Taji learned the Dragon moves. It's a new partnership, in China at least. But I'm sure we won't find any allies among our enemies in the Dragon Ryu when we return to the Tateyama Mountains.

Sensei passes a tray of acupuncture needles to Master Jang. He shakes his head.

"You can do it this time, Ki-Yaga. And we will use Lu Zeng's diagram to check the placement lines."

Sensei inserts two more thin silver needles in Yoshi's wrist. I flinch, but Yoshi doesn't react at all. He is beyond feeling more pain.

Master Jang then opens Yoshi's mouth, places a ball of paste inside, and moves Yoshi's jaw open and shut. Yoshi swallows and sputters. Master Jang might be a good cook, but it seems that his medicines taste awful.

Suddenly, Yoshi opens his eyes to find us all watching.

"What did I miss?" he asks, his voice hoarse.

No one is sure what to say.

He groans. "My finger hurts."

I want to be the one to comfort Yoshi, but I can't find the right words. My brain is empty.

Look in your heart, Sensei reminds me.

"You had an accident, but you're okay now. A poisoned

dart pierced your forefinger. Your finger is gone now. But the poison is, too," I blurt out.

"My finger is gone?" Surprised, Yoshi notices his bandaged hand and the needles in his wrist.

Kyoko gently closes her hand over his. "I have six fingers and you have four. Together we have exactly the right number."

"That's all right, then." Yoshi smiles and closes his eyes to sleep.

Master Jang extracts the needles, returning them to the tray. "My work is done," he says. "I have helped increase Yoshi's *ki,* and now he must fight his own battle against whatever poison has leaked into his body."

Yoshi has always been a great fighter. But his true strength is not in his arms and legs. It is in his heart. When he accidentally killed his childhood friend, he learned to live again. When he blamed himself for Captain Oong's drowning, he found a way out of the darkness. And with our help, he'll survive this, too.

Master Jang has his dagger in hand again. "It is time for payment to be made."

Kneeling before Master Jang, Kyoko holds her hair up in a ponytail, neck bared before his blade.

I hold my breath as the Poisoner raises his weapon. It's razor sharp. If he misses by even a little, Kyoko might lose her head.

The blade falls with a sinister hiss of metal fighting its way through air. Kyoko's head is now covered in wisps of hair as white as smoke.

"How do I look?" she asks.

She looks more like a snow monkey than ever.

"You look like Kyoko," says Sensei.

"You look no different to me," Taji agrees.

They're both right. Hair doesn't matter at all. In China, they believe hair is a gift from your parents, so it is disrespectful to cut it off. But Kyoko has given hers as a gift to save a friend's life. That's much more important. And she hasn't got any parents, anyway.

Grinning, Kyoko runs her fingers through her newly short hair. "At least no one will be able to pull my hair anymore." She wrinkles her nose at me.

Yoshi groans, shifting uncomfortably in his sleep.

"I won't leave you, Yoshi," I whisper in his ear.

"There is nothing to do now but sit and wait," says Master Jang.

Sensei doesn't sit. He paces the wooden floor. Back

and forth, forth and back. His knuckles white, hands clenched around the hilt of the *wodao* dagger Master Jang gave him.

"If Yoshi has lost a finger, then so shall Lu Zeng," he announces.

"But Sensei, you taught us it is not an eye for an eye or a finger for a finger," I say.

"No. Little Cockroach, you are right. But Lu Zeng did not want Yoshi's finger. He wanted not only my life but the lives of all my students. And I cannot let such a dishonorable deed pass unpunished. It is the way of the warrior. Lu Zeng must lose a finger, too."

"We're coming with you," says Mikko.

Taji, Kyoko, and I stand beside him.

"We leave Yoshi in your safe hands." Sensei bows to Master Jang.

"I am pleased to see that you have already found a good use for your *wodao*." The Poisoner smiles.

"Perhaps I should stay." I hesitate at the door. I've already let Yoshi down so many times.

"Go. I'll take your place at Yoshi's side," says a voice beside me.

"Chen!" I'm always pleased to see him but now more than any other time.

"That boy," huffs Master Jang. "Ever since I saved his life, I can't get rid of him. 'Haven't you got a home to go to?' I say."

But Chen hasn't got a home, and Master Jang knows that. That's why he doesn't turn Chen away. But this time it is us who need him. With a last look at Yoshi and Chen sitting by his side, I hop after Sensei and my friends.

When Sensei is in a hurry, he is very hard to keep up with. Long strides cover the distance to the Forbidden City gates in record time. He sweeps away all before him like a monsoon. The crowd parts as he rushes on with his staff held high.

At the gate, he waves his jade seal and the soldiers gesture us through. There is no time to admire the sculptures and stand on the bridge looking into the water. Sensei is a man driven by a wind more powerful than dragon's breath. By the time we reach Lu Zeng's palace, I am gasping for air and leaning on Mikko for support.

"Stop!" The guard at the entrance is paying attention this time. He learned the lesson Mikko taught him.

But Sensei is not in the mood for discussion. With one foot, he knocks the lance from the man's hand, and with the other, he sends him crashing to the floor.

"Did you see that?" Kyoko whistles.

"I didn't," says Taji. "But it sounded like Sensei flattened someone."

"It took Sensei only two kicks," I say to Taji, then look at the man lying prone. "Our master is very angry."

Already, Sensei is storming though the courtyard garden, yelling for Lu Zeng. "Where are you hiding now? You who are less than slug slime on the bottom of my sandals!"

At home, Onaku the Sword Master tells us stories about the legendary Ki-Yaga, who swept like a roaring torrent across the battlefield, but the master we know is a man of peace. He sits calmly in the eye of the storm, going with the flow. But not today. Today he rages like a river in flood.

"You can't enter this house uninvited." Six guards bar his way.

"I do not have time to play with toy soldiers!" our teacher bellows.

You cannot swim against a raging river, and no man can stand against Sensei now. The guards are fools to try.

With a sharp crack, Sensei brings his traveling staff down on the head of the middle guard. The man falls with a thump. Unrelenting, the staff flies upward under the chin of another, who collapses over the body of his friend. Sensei is leaving a trail of sore heads behind him. Sword in one hand, staff in the other, he holds the remaining guards at a distance as he barges into the Room of Science.

And now it is our turn to practice.

"Our master's business is private," says Taji as we step in between the guards and Sensei.

"I'm not fighting a blind kid," says one guard.

"And we're not fighting a girl, either," says another.

"Then that will make our task easier. I don't care who I fight." Taji swings his sword, and three guards are left standing weaponless. Kyoko has her dagger against the fourth's neck.

"Drop it," she snarls.

There's no one left for Mikko and me to fight. So we gather up the swords while Kyoko ties the men in a bundle.

"Now that is a much better use for knots," I say, grinning.

Inside the room, Sensei is still shouting. The walls shake with the anger of his *ki*.

"Show yourself, Lu Zeng! You are no scholar! Your brain is filled with tortoise drool."

We try not to giggle. But it's an insult Lu Zeng cannot ignore. He bursts into the room.

"What are you doing here?" Lu Zeng stabs his forefinger into Sensei's chest.

He shouldn't do that. His finger is in enough danger already.

"A man of honor does not send assassins against children," says Sensei.

"Children." Lu Zeng snorts. "Your students could easily disarm and kill ten of the Emperor's soldiers. It is a fair game."

"The game was already over!" Sensei rears like a phoenix from the ashes, breathing fire. "My students are under my protection. You have offended the honor of the Cockroach Ryu, and I have come to exact restitution."

The air bristles the way it does before a great storm. Sensei's voice roars like thunder. Lightning is about to strike.

"Guards!" Lu Zeng yells.

Sensei grins. "You were right about one thing. My students can easily disarm a troop of the Emperor's guards. Even those assigned to the Imperial Rites Secretary."

For a brief moment, a look of panic crosses Lu Zeng's face. Then haughty disdain replaces it.

"We will draw our swords and fight," he says. "I do not need help to beat you. You are an old man, whereas I have benefited from my studies. I have the body of someone half your age. My arms and legs have the strength of those of a young warrior."

Foolish Lu Zeng. It doesn't matter what shape his body is in. Sensei has a mind like a steel trap, and Lu Zeng will soon find his limbs caught in it.

Our master draws his *wodao*. The metal gleams.

Sensei prefers not to fight with a blade anymore. Too dangerous, he says. People get hurt. He uses his traveling staff as a *bo.* It's all he ever needs to win. But this time Sensei doesn't want to win. He wants to slice.

Sensei steps forward, swinging his blade in a great arc. Lu Zeng blocks, pushing our teacher back. As Sensei pushes forward again, Lu Zeng slowly circles the room.

"What is he doing?" Mikko asks.

"Strategy." Kyoko frowns. "He's heading for the door."

"He's running away?" Mikko is stunned.

But it doesn't surprise me. The Spider is looking for a hole to crawl into.

Lu Zeng backs out the door, but Sensei follows after him, down the hall and outside.

A crowd of palace folk soon gathers.

Watch this, Sensei whispers inside my head. Intrigued, the White Crane raises its head.

Slowly, Sensei lifts one leg and tucks it behind the other. Shaolin white crane. He whirls, faster and faster. Lu Zeng's sword skids across the dirt and is quickly swallowed by the crowd. I'm sure it will be sold on the street and will put many meals on someone's table.

"Don't kill me," Lu Zeng begs, dropping to his knees.

"Give me your hand," Sensei says.

Sensei steps forward, swinging
his blade in a great arc.

Relieved, Lu Zeng holds out his hand, and Sensei helps him rise.

I can see the look on Lu Zeng's face. He thinks he's fooled Sensei again. He's expecting a truce.

But Sensei doesn't let go. Raising the *wodao,* our master slices the index finger from Lu Zeng's hand.

"Now you are the same as my student," Sensei says. "Honor is restored, and our differences are resolved."

But I don't think Lu Zeng heard any of that. He's too busy yelling.

"What's this?" A big soldier pushes his way through the crowd.

Leave me now, Sensei says. *I must do this on my own.*

With a gentle elbow, I signal to Mikko to drop back. I nudge Taji, and the message passes to Kyoko, and by then we have melted into the edge of the crowd, just as Big Wu taught us. We can barely see Sensei, but we can still hear everything.

"It's his fault, Captain!" Lu Zeng whines.

He has no finger to point with, but he waves his arm at Sensei. "He mutilated my hand." The crowd gasps at the bloody stump.

"Is this true?" the captain demands.

"Yes," says Sensei. "It was payment owed. His finger was forfeited to me."

Lu Zeng lunges at Sensei, but another soldier holds him back.

"Do you know who I am?" Lu Zeng demands, shoving the soldier's arm away.

"Yes," says the captain. "And I know this man, too. He entered the main Outer City Gate a few days ago. When a scholar of the first order and an imperial government minister fight, it is a matter for the Emperor to decide."

"You're in big trouble now, Ki-Yaga," says Lu Zeng, sneering. "It's against the law to dissect a human being."

He should know.

"That's enough talk," orders the captain. "If you both behave yourselves, I won't need to bind and gag you."

"Do you think Sensei might be thrown in prison?" Kyoko looks worried as she watches the soldiers lead Sensei and Lu Zeng away from us.

"No prison can hold our teacher," says Taji. "I bet he did this on purpose."

Rescue the boy, Sensei whispers.

"I think you are right, Taji," I say. "Now that Lu Zeng is not in his palace, it will be easier to rescue Enlai."

"Good thinking." Mikko slaps me on the back.

It wasn't really my idea, but I'm happy to take the credit.

"And now we might have to rescue Sensei, too," worries Kyoko.

"That's okay," Mikko says. "We've done that before, and we can do it again."

The crowd disperses, leaving us standing in the street alone.

Not quite. There's a tug at my sleeve.

"What are you doing here?" I ask. The Forbidden City is always closed to commoners like Chen. It's an offense punishable by death.

"Yoshi is awake. He has been calling for you," he says.

For now, nothing else matters. Even Sensei must wait.

CHAPTER THIRTEEN

礼

DRAGON
THRONE

"I'm coming," Yoshi insists. "I'm strong enough. The poison is beaten."

I want Yoshi with us, but more than that, I want him well. "Wouldn't it be better for you to rest?" I ask.

He shakes his head. "Master Jang said I should exercise my muscles and not just sit around."

It's settled then. Rescuing Enlai will be excellent exercise. Just what the doctor ordered.

Beijing is a city afraid of strangers. No one is allowed out after dark. Using the techniques we learned from the Lin, we creep along the familiar route to Lu Zeng's palace. The moon winks and hides behind a cloud. It's on our team too.

"All clear," barks the soldier on patrol.

They search the streets, enforcing the Emperor's curfew. Making sure everyone is indoors. Anyone out on the street is instantly under suspicion. An enemy spy.

The soldier's red lanterns cast an eerie glow.

"We need one of those lights," I whisper.

"You could get it. Do the finger thing," suggests Mikko.

I shrug. "I'm not sure if I can. I'll try, but we need a backup plan."

I look at Yoshi. He'll think of one.

"Well . . ." He smiles. "If it doesn't work, Mikko can just hit him over the head with the flat of his sword. We already know that's very effective."

"It's how we got into Lu Zeng's house the first time," Taji explains to Kyoko.

I choose a soldier about the same height as me. An easy reach.

"Help me!" Kyoko cries. The soldier turns toward her and starts over. "Help, help!"

Stepping behind him, I press my fingers hard against his neck. He collapses like a clump of sticky rice.

"Is that what happened to me?" asks Kyoko, picking up the soldier's lantern and handing it to me.

Yes, except Kyoko fell like a shower of cherry blossoms.

"Sorry about that." I grin.

"You are not," she says, swiping at my head. "But I'm glad you did it. You're very clever, Niya."

In the darkness, my face is as red as the lantern.

At the door to Lu Zeng's palace, I stop. "Wait," I say.

"What?" asks Kyoko.

"Before we do this, I want to say something impor-tant. In front of everyone. I want to apologize to Yoshi." I turn to him. "I'm sorry I didn't trust you. I was stupid, foolish —"

"It's okay," interrupts Yoshi. "You don't have to say anything more."

"But I'm enjoying it," says Mikko. "Particularly the part about how stupid Niya can be."

Yoshi and I both lunge at Mikko, but he darts away. It's hard to catch a gecko, especially at night.

There are no guards, but the doors are bolted firmly. Nine bolts across. Nine bolts down.

"I wish Chen were here," I say. "He'd be able to pick these locks." I look around hopefully. He's always popping up. But not this time.

"Move aside." Kyoko pushes me out of the way. "This is a job for my fingers."

Kyoko jiggles and twists, wriggles and lifts. The first bolt slides out. Once, twice . . . eighteen times.

We step through the door, into a place far blacker than the night outside.

"Follow me. I'll lead the way to the Room of Science," says Taji. Of course, the Golden Bat doesn't need a lantern to see. I point the beam in the direction of his voice and we all follow.

"Enlai!" Kyoko calls. "I've come back. Like I promised."

No answer.

"Enlai!" Yoshi bellows.

Still no answer.

Where is he? Without a voice, he can't respond, but if his hands or feet are free, then he can tap. Or knock. We stop to listen, looking at Taji, who listens deepest of all.

He shakes his head. Sometimes silence is so loud you can't hear anything else.

"This place is full of secret walls and cupboards," says Kyoko. "It's hopeless. We'll never find him."

The Lin couldn't find him, either.

He might not even be here. Worse than that, he might already be dead.

Kyoko sniffs. She's probably thinking the same thing.

Oh, Enlai, where are you?

I am here, he answers.

"What's wrong?" Mikko asks, seeing the surprise on my face.

"I thought I heard something," I say.

No one speaks. We're all listening as hard as we can.

Where are you? I call.

Tortoise Room.

"I think I know where he is!" I shout. "This way."

No one asks how I know. They just hurry along the corridor behind me, Kyoko running fastest.

I stop at the door to the Tortoise Room.

"It makes sense," says Taji. "This is the room where Lu Zeng keeps his most important treasures."

And it's not far from the Room of Experiments. I shudder.

I am here! I am here! the voice babbles excitedly.

I put my hands over my ears.

"Are you all right?" Kyoko asks this time.

"I thought I heard something again." I shake my head from side to side.

"It's okay." Kyoko puts her arm around me. "You're doing your best. It's not like you can hear his voice in your head."

I can, I want to tell her. But I have learned secrets have a time and place. I can't share this one yet.

Here I am! Enlai calls.

I trace his voice with the lantern beam. The White Crane's eyes pick out the small cracks that give the hiding place away.

"There is a door in the wall." I point halfway up to the ceiling.

"You always have the best eyesight," Yoshi says, admiring.

"Show-off," teases Taji.

If only they knew.

But now we have another problem. There's no ladder. Kyoko could easily climb up to Enlai, but how could she get him down? We need a rope.

"If you cannot see the answer, you must look inside yourself," Sensei teaches.

Or maybe inside your jacket pocket.

"I know," I say. "We'll use our headbands to make a rope. Kyoko can anchor it to the door in the wall and then help Enlai climb down it."

Mikko grins as he hands his headband to Kyoko. "Lu Zeng was right about your knots being useful."

Expertly, she ties our headbands together. She places

the rope in her mouth and picks her way up the wall, finding handholds in the uneven stone. Only the Snow Monkey could do that.

A soft click and the door is unlatched.

"Here I am, Enlai," Kyoko says. "I promised I would return. I've brought a rescue team with me."

A small head pokes out into the lantern light. A small hand waves.

"Let's go!" calls Taji. "I don't want to stay any longer than we have to."

He hates it here. We all do.

Kyoko clambers down with the boy clinging to her back like a baby monkey.

At the door she carefully relocks the bolts to hide the evidence of our visit. Immediately, a large shape detaches from the shadows. It's Big Wu. When Yoshi places Enlai in his arms, the final debt is paid.

"We are leaving tonight," Big Wu says. "The Emperor will hear your master's case in the Hall of Middle Harmony tomorrow. Good luck. I will always think of you."

Like a ghostly demon, he fades into the night.

We're on our own. Even Sensei is not here.

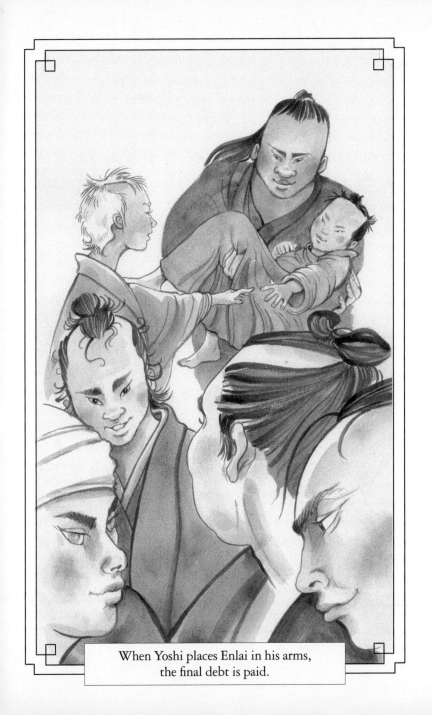

When Yoshi places Enlai in his arms,
the final debt is paid.

In the morning, we rise early. There is something in the marketplace I want, but it's not breakfast. I'm too nervous to eat.

"It's time to collect Sensei's new robe," I say.

Taji leads the way, easily sorting one street from another.

"There's the fountain." Mikko points.

"And there's the old man, waiting for us," says Yoshi.

As I approach, the street vendor holds out a package.

"Thank you." I bow. "But I must tell you we have already been paid for rescuing the boy. Elder Lin has provided us with special lessons."

"I know that, and it is a rare opportunity to be used well. But a boy has two grandfathers, and I must pay my own debt."

He turns and walks away, leaving us to puzzle over the strange ways of the Lin.

"What was that all about?" asks Kyoko.

"When we first came to Beijing, he spoke to me in the

street," I explain. "He promised me a wonderful robe for Sensei after we rescued the boy."

"We thought he meant you," says Yoshi.

Kyoko straightens her shoulders indignantly. "I don't look like a boy."

"You do now." For once, Mikko dodges just in time.

On the way to the Forbidden City gate, I walk beside Yoshi. "Let's never argue again. I am so glad you didn't tell me about Mei and Du Feng." My voice shakes. "I would have betrayed them."

"No one is perfect, Niya. Not even you." He pokes me in the ribs. "I had no choice but to keep the information secret."

Yoshi is much wiser than me. He trusted Sensei from the beginning.

"I'm such an idiot," I say.

"Do you know how long I've waited to hear that?" Yoshi grins.

"I'm going to tell Sensei, too. As soon as we see him."

I heard, he whispers. Inside my head, Sensei is grinning, too. *You always know how to make me smile, Niya. I need that.*

I smile back.

It's going to be a long day, but it's off to a good start.

Bells ring out to announce that the Emperor is holding court. A crowd of senior officials has gathered to see the Jin Shi from Japan and catch a glimpse of the Emperor on his throne.

"I heard he injured the Esteemed Secretary," whispers a man beside me.

"You cannot trust foreigners," says his friend.

Wedged into the corner, we hope no one will notice us and send us out. We have no friends here to defend us. Master Jang and Big Wu have returned with the Lin to the forest. Only Chen remains, and he is not allowed inside the Forbidden City gates.

But Sensei's presence always commands respect. He raises his traveling staff and bows to the audience.

Bang, bang.

A gong sounds. The Secretary for Justice, a tall man in a blue robe and a Wu Sha hat, speaks first. "The Dragon Throne will hear the complaint of Lord Lu Zeng, Esteemed Secretary of the Board of Rites."

Sensei doesn't even get a mention.

Behind the Secretary for Justice, the Emperor sits on a great throne flanked by golden dragon pillars. Smoke from the unicorn incense burners creates a thin screen between the Son of Heaven and the descendants of mere mortals.

"Look what he did to my finger." Lu Zeng waves his hand.

"I do not see any finger," Sensei says solemnly.

In the crowd, someone snickers. Then a wave of laughter erupts. Even the Emperor smiles.

"This man is a threat to our city and the whole of the Middle Kingdom," insists Lu Zeng.

The Secretary for Justice gestures to Sensei to respond.

"The only person I am threatening is Lu Zeng. First, he kidnapped my student and then a young boy."

"If it's true, let him prove it." Lu Zeng smirks. "Make him produce the boy and we'll hear what he has to say."

Lu Zeng is very clever. He knows it can't be done. Even if we have found Enlai, he knows the Lin will have already moved him to a safe place outside the city.

"Produce the boy," commands the Emperor.

"I cannot," Sensei says. "But I can produce my student."

"Perhaps there is no boy," Lu Zeng sneers.

"He's lying," Kyoko calls. "I know because he kidnapped me."

All eyes turn to us. So much for staying unnoticed.

Still Lu Zeng smiles. He doesn't think the testimony of one girl will count. But he doesn't know Kyoko. Even the Emperor will be silk string in her fingers.

Surprised, the Emperor gestures for a guard to escort Kyoko forward. "Is it true you kidnapped a girl?" he asks Lu Zeng.

"I am accomplished with a sword, Your Excellency," Kyoko interrupts. "I can take care of myself—except when three men sneak in the dark. But," she whispers conspiratorially, "at least I bit two of them."

Kyoko is doing it again. Wrapping even the Emperor of the Dragon Throne around her finger.

"What happened to your hair?" the Emperor asks, easily distracted. "Hair is a gift from your parents. It should be treasured."

"It was. I sacrificed my hair to save my friend's life. Lu Zeng poisoned him," says Kyoko.

"You are brave and beautiful. Would you like to

be a Chinese princess?" the Emperor asks, completely forgetting why he is here.

I understand that. I forget things when Kyoko speaks to me, too.

Kyoko looks thoughtful. Is she really thinking about staying? I feel as if a sword has been run through my stomach. But I remember what Chen taught me. If you love something, you must let it go.

"How many wives have you got?" queries Kyoko.

"One hundred and fifty-six," replies the Emperor. "But they are not all first-rank wives."

"And what number would I be?" Kyoko asks.

The Emperor gestures to a scribe who does a quick calculation.

"Number sixty-three, tenth rank," the scribe announces.

That will never do. Kyoko does not even like to come second.

The Snow Monkey is grinning now. I breathe a sigh of relief. She's not going anywhere.

"No, thank you," Kyoko tells the Emperor. "I do not wish to be a middle-order princess."

No longer playful, the Emperor looks angry. Why is it that as soon as something cannot be had, everyone wants it? The Emperor wants Kyoko.

Sensei quickly intervenes. "The girl is not a suitable wife for your Lordship. Hold up your hands, Kyoko."

"I see." The Emperor looks disappointed. "I am sorry I cannot accept your student as my wife. All my princesses must be perfect."

Kyoko is perfect, but I'm glad the Emperor can't see it.

And she's smart, too. She plays along, following Sensei's lead.

"It was an honor to be considered. I'm sure your palace is wonderful to behold and your princesses are very fortunate." She pauses. "Unlike me, when I was caged in Lu Zeng's palace."

"You put this girl in a cage?" the Emperor demands of Lu Zeng.

"Not just me," Kyoko says. "The boy too. Lu Zeng was going to cut him open. Of course, I would have stopped him."

"You?" The Emperor is intrigued now.

"I am dangerous with a sword, remember?" She pulls a dagger from her *obi*.

A guard rushes forward, but the Emperor waves him back, laughing. "I am glad I do not have a knife-wielding princess. I would be too frightened to sleep at night. But I see your teacher has taught you well."

"Not just me." Kyoko waves, and we move forward to stand with her.

The Emperor looks bemused. Taji's sightless eyes, Mikko's one arm, my one leg. Yoshi towering over us.

"Do you have anything more to add?" the Emperor asks Sensei.

"Show him, Yoshi," our master instructs.

Yoshi holds up his hand. The bandage is bloody where the wound has seeped.

"Lu Zeng tried to poison all my students. A Plum Flower Sleeve Arrow dart grazed this boy's finger. It had to be cut off," says Sensei.

The Emperor's eyes move to Kyoko's dagger. Perhaps he thinks she did it. Our cheeky monkey grins.

"I am tired," the Emperor says suddenly. "And hungry. I have wasted enough time today. Lu Zeng is hereby stripped of office and sent to prison. But I do not like disturbances in my streets either, so Jin Shi Ki-Yaga must leave the Middle Kingdom and take his students with him." He rises from the throne. "Now, where is my lunch?"

"Lord Dragon Emperor." Sensei kneels, head to the floor. "One more thing."

"Yes." The Emperor turns, irritated.

"I have a message for you from my Lord Emperor in Japan."

"Ah." The Emperor smiles. "I should spend more time in correspondence with my friend." He reaches for the message scroll in Sensei's hand. "I will write to my friend in Japan after my meal. I remember now that I have heard an interesting story about you." The Emperor stares at Sensei, his attention rekindled. "I heard you defeated one of my best soldiers, Qing-Shen. I am impressed."

"It is my student who deserves your praise." Sensei gestures to Yoshi.

"It is said Qing-Shen was once your student, too. And that you were tutor to the royal children of Japan."

Sensei nods.

"You must be a very good teacher," the Emperor says, still studying Sensei.

I don't like the sound of this. I fear that at any moment, the Son of Heaven will decide his children, too, deserve such a teacher.

The gong sounds again. Somewhere lunch is ready, and the audience is over.

"Tomorrow we will discuss this further. Come to the Hall of Complete Harmony and show the soldier on duty your seal," the Emperor orders.

Trumpets sound, and everyone rises as the Emperor departs.

"What if he wants you to stay?" I ask.

Sensei shakes his head. "I am leaving China very soon."

"We're all leaving together, aren't we?" Kyoko asks, remembering how Nezume stayed to teach the Japanese prince.

"Yes. This Emperor's time is almost over, and our time is yet to come. Our destiny lies back in Japan. When we return, the Cockroach Ryu must be ready to fight a great battle."

"Even Nezume?" Yoshi asks.

"All of us. If it is necessary."

We walk in silence. Every day a samurai trains to fight. But Sensei has taught us never to fight unless we absolutely have to. It must be something very important.

Sensei looks sad.

At least we'll be together, I say.

Inside my head his voice is barely a whisper. *Yes. But I do not know if we will all fight on the same side.*

I shiver. Once I would have argued, refused to believe that could ever be true. But already I have betrayed Yoshi's friendship once.

"What's wrong, Niya?" Yoshi booms in my ear.

"I'm c-cold," I stammer.

"I can fix that." He wraps his arms around my shoulders until I feel warm.

CHAPTER FOURTEEN

勇

YIN AND YANG

"We will leave tonight, but I would like one last look at Lu Zeng's palace before we go," says Sensei.

"Why?" Kyoko shudders. "I never want to see that place again."

But the palace pulls us to it. Cruel fingers of memory snake and tug. As we grow nearer, even Kyoko walks faster.

"Are you all right?" I ask.

"Yes," she says, her teeth clenched and her jaw drawn tight. "I think I might throw a few rocks."

Mikko stumbles, scrabbling inside his sandal. "Here's a stone to get you started."

"Not stones," she says. "I want to throw huge rocks. I want to smash everything to bits."

That's not like Kyoko at all. She likes to throw things but only to tease us or score a point in a competition. Never to destroy.

The building looms black and foreboding, a great tombstone monument to the graveyard inside. Overhead the clouds gather, obscuring the moon and deepening the darkness.

"It might rain tonight," Sensei says.

Even the Dragon cries tears over Lu Zeng's palace.

Sensei wedges his traveling staff into the ground. "There is one only thing that thrives inside these walls. Great evil. Lu Zeng grows more powerful and more wicked every day."

"But not now that he's in prison," says Mikko.

"Bars cannot hold a man like Lu Zeng. Not for long. The palace will draw him back. Darkness feeds on darkness. This is a place where monsters are made."

My friends and I often tell horror stories to tease each other while we walk, tales of giant *oni* and water beast *kappa.* We won't be doing that anymore. Now we know monsters are real. And human.

"I wish I could burn this place down," I mutter. "When we played the Game of Five Elements, Chen taught us that fire beats wood. But even better, flames eat darkness."

Yoshi puts his hand on my shoulder. "We could do it, you know. No one is here to stop us."

"What? Burn it down?" Kyoko's eyes are already flaming. I can see she wants to.

"But someone might get hurt," says Mikko.

I shake my head. "With all the water vats every-where, the fire will be put out well before it causes any other damage. Lu Zeng's palace will be ash and cinders, but the surrounding buildings will be safe."

"They look empty anyway," Yoshi says. "No one would choose to live near this place."

"Lu Zeng has a lot of animals in there. Not just tortoises. We'll need to release them first." Kyoko is already making a plan.

"That's good," says Taji. "I hate to think what Lu Zeng intends to do with those poor creatures."

We look to Sensei for approval.

He raises his staff high. "Tonight Lu Zeng's palace will cease to exist."

With practiced fingers, Kyoko unbolts the door. We follow Taji through the darkness, past the garden with its false promise of peace and tranquility.

"We need some light," Sensei says when we reach the Room of Science.

He raises the blinds, stretching his hands toward the sky. In answer, the moon reappears.

"Did you see that?" I whisper to Mikko.

"Coincidence." He giggles.

But I know it's not. There are great forces at work in this room tonight, and I'm relieved that not all of them are bad.

"There are four hatchways to the animal compounds. One in each corner of the room," says Kyoko.

Lu Zeng's evil stretches in all directions.

"And there are cages in the roof," she adds.

His wickedness even reaches toward Heaven.

"How will we get up there?" Mikko asks.

"The same way Lu Zeng did." Kyoko pulls on a silk tassel, and a rope ladder drops from the ceiling. "I never thought I would gladly climb up here again."

The thin rope swings and sways beneath her weight. I can't bear to look.

Luckily, there is no time for standing around gazing skyward.

"Niya, Mikko, and Taji will release the animals from the holding compounds while Kyoko frees the birds in the roof. Yoshi and I will rescue the tortoises," Sensei says.

There was a time when I might have felt a twinge of

jealousy, watching Sensei leave with Yoshi. But we all have our own special talents. And Yoshi is the only one strong enough to carry the oldest tortoise.

We locate and unlatch the cages one by one. The room is a flurry of wings and a scuttle of feet.

"Shoo, shoo." Kyoko herds bats, parrots, eagles, and sparrows toward the window. I open the door for cats, dogs, and monkeys. Some of the snakes look dangerous, so we carry their cages outside. Yoshi sits the great tortoise beside them.

"Will they be all right here?" I ask.

"We all have to find our own way, whether we swim, fly, or plod step by step," says Sensei. "And wherever they go, they will be much better off than where they were."

I can't argue with that.

"It won't be long before the animals attract attention," warns Yoshi.

It's time to act.

Sensei takes Lu Zeng's cylinder from his pocket and removes the scroll with the Twelve Symbols of Sovereignty painted on it. "The scroll is valuable," he says, tucking the parchment inside his jacket. "But this cylinder is worthless. Perhaps you can put it to good use, Mikko."

I smile. The cylinder is made of silk and gold. To most people, it's worth a fortune. But Sensei is right. Mikko will find a much better use for it.

Mikko rummages in his pocket and extracts the bag of black powder his Owl Ninja tutor gave him. He tips some into the cylinder. "I need something to plug the end with."

"I've got just the thing." Kyoko pulls a tangled string of monkey-fist knots from her pocket. "I don't want to see any of these for a long time."

Sensei ties the cylinder to an arrow and hands it me. "You are our best archer, Niya. Aim true and land it in the center of the roof."

I fit the arrow to my bow. I draw back the string.

And then I hope. Not even the White Crane can track an arrow's flight in the darkness.

Pfft. It falls with a gentle thud onto the palace roof.

"Dead center," announces Taji.

Bang. The cylinder makes its own announcement. Sparks spit and sputter. A huge sound-and-light display is about to begin.

Not even the White Crane can track an
arrow's flight in the darkness.

"I'm going to enjoy these fireworks," says Mikko.

Me too. After their work is done, there will be one less dark, frightening corner in the Middle Kingdom.

The flames are small at first. No one notices them lick and slither across the rooftop. Soon the whole building is ablaze.

"There is nothing as pleasantly warming as a night fire," Sensei says, smiling while Lu Zeng's palace burns.

Around us, the pathways fill with people. Nearby buildings empty into orderly processions of servants carrying cloths and half-finished meals, princesses hobbling on bound feet, and old men with pipes in their mouths.

Soldiers form lines, passing buckets of water from hand to hand, using the water from the vats to control the fire. No one is in danger here. The only thing lost tonight will be Lu Zeng's work. And no one needs that.

It's a time for celebration. Mikko hands Sensei the package.

"What's this?" Sensei asks.

"It is a gift from all of us," I say.

"But what is it for?" Sensei fumbles to untie the string. Even he has trouble with Kyoko's knots.

I can tell he is pleased. Everyone likes to get a present. Even a legendary samurai warrior.

"It is not my birthday," Sensei says, pulling the wrapping apart.

The blue robe falls, billowing like ocean waves, and the Twelve Symbols of Sovereignty gleam in the firelight. The *fu* symbol, for the balance between good and evil, glows brightest of all.

"This robe is for a time much more important than a birthday," I say. "This is for the time you told us about. When everything will be made right again. When all past mistakes are erased."

Is it my imagination, or is the symbol for evil a little brighter? Perhaps Sensei will need all the help he can get in the days to come.

I suspect I will, he whispers inside my head.

And when you do, I will be there with you. I promise.

The flames illuminate Sensei's smiling face.

I have always known that, he says.

"Every man, grab a bucket," calls a soldier.

We edge away. We don't want to do anything to help them slow the flames. We want the palace to be soot and rubble.

Nobody notices as we make our way through the pathways and the battery of side gates. A misty rain drapes over our departure. We are leaving Beijing and never coming back. Sensei stops, looking back toward where the fire still burns. "Yin and yang. Good and evil. Dark and light." He sighs. "There will never be one without the other. But we can always choose where we wish to be."

"I don't wish to be here. Let's go, Master," Yoshi says, tugging at Sensei's sleeve. "The soldiers will be looking for us by now."

"Just a moment," Sensei replies.

"We may not have a moment. What are we waiting for?" I ask.

"Hello, friend samurai," says a voice beside me.

Chen has a small bag strapped to his back and new shoes on his feet. Walking shoes.

"Now we can go," announces Sensei. "I like your shoes," he tells Chen. "I believe you could walk to Japan in a fine pair of shoes like that."

"Thank you, Master." Chen bows.

Now Sensei has one more student.

"I thought you wanted to see the Great Wall before we went home," says Mikko.

"Maybe we will," says Sensei. "But a path will not always go where I want it to."

Somewhere along the wall, a nightingale trills softly.

"A bird does not sing because it has an answer," Sensei says.

"It sings because it has a song," Kyoko finishes the line for him.

And the White Crane doesn't fly because it knows where it is going. It soars because it has wings.

Sometimes things just happen because they can.

"Race you," Yoshi challenges.

Our feet fly after him.

THE SEVEN VIRTUES OF BUSHIDO

義　勇　仁　礼　真　名誉　忠誠

	GI	rectitude
	YU	courage
	JIN	benevolence
	REI	respect
	MAKOTO	honesty
	MEIYO	honor
	CHUSEI	loyalty

USEFUL WORDS

ACONITE	poisonous plant
BO	wooden stick used as a weapon
CHI, JIN, YU	wisdom, benevolence, and courage
FU	Chinese symbol for the balance between good and evil
JIN SHI	title recognizing achievement in the Imperial Examinations
MANDARIN	high-ranking Chinese offical
ONI	an ogre-like monster
RYU	school
SENSEI	teacher
SHAKUHACHI	a bamboo flute
TENGU	a mountain goblin priest able to change into a black crow
TSUZUMI	traditional Japanese drum
WODAO	sword similar to a *katana*

ACKNOWLEDGMENTS

It's fun to write. My imagination takes me places my feet probably never will. But writing is also a lot of hard work for all those people who support me every word of the way: My boys, Jackson and Cassidy. Di Bates, who inspires me. Bill Condon, Vicki Stanton, Barbara Brown, Sally Hall, and Mo Johnson. Every book, I say thank you. Every time, I am grateful that some things never change.

To my editor, Sue Whiting, who rescues me from the bottom of deep plot holes and is a geography whiz, too. I am literally lost without you to help me find my bearings. To Virginia Grant, who single-handedly wrestles present participles to the ground. To Rhian, whose artwork brings magic to every chapter. To the wonderful team at Walker Books. Thank you all.